W9-AYG-548

ATTICUS
OF ROME
30 B.C.

❖ ◆ ❖ ◆ ❖

THE LIFE AND TIMES

ATTICUS OF ROME

30 B.C.

❖ ✦ ❖ ✦ ❖

BY BARRY DENENBERG

Scholastic Inc. New York

Copyright © 2004 by Barry Denenberg

Library of Congress Cataloging-in-Publication Data

Denenberg, Barry.
Atticus of Rome: Rome 30 B.C. / by Barry Denenberg. — 1st ed.
p. cm. — (Life and Times)

Summary: In ancient Rome, Atticus, a young slave purchased by a
wealthy and powerful lawyer, finds that he is completely invisible to the
people from whom he must gather information in order to help foil a
plot against the Emperor.
ISBN 0-439-52453-9
1. Rome — History — Nero, 54–68 — Juvenile fiction.
[1. Rome — History — Nero, 54–68 — Fiction.
2. Slavery — Fiction.   3. Spies — Fiction.]
I. Title.   II. Series.
PZ7.D4135At 2004
[Fic]—dc22   2003026091

10 9 8 7 6 5 4 3 2 1   04 05 06 07 08

The text type in this book was set in Mrs. Eaves.
The display type was set in Exocet.
Book design by Elizabeth B. Parisi

Printed in the U.S.A.
First edition, October 2004

ACKNOWLEDGMENTS

The author would like to thank Kerry Blassone,
Amy Griffin, Beth Levine, Liz Usuriello, Terra McEvoy,
and everyone at Scholastic.

CAST OF CHARACTERS

❖ ◆ ❖ ◆ ❖

Atticus: a twelve-year-old slave boy

Lucius Opimius: an influential political figure; friend and confidant of the Emperor; Atticus's master

Cassius Macedo: Lucius Opimius's personal physician

Lady Claudia: Lucius Opimius's young (fifteen-year-old) second wife

Aristide: Lucius Opimius's trusted astrologer

Galerius Traculus: a wealthy and ambitious real estate developer

General Marius Maximus: a popular Roman general

Caius Curtius: a highly respected Roman senator

Quintas Crassus: owner of a famous gladiatorial school

A Smell Darker
and More Threatening
than Animal Terror

❖ ◆ ❖ ◆ ❖

Last night, Atticus had had the dream again.

At the beginning of the dream, the sky was clear blue and the midday sun was unbearably hot. But now, later in the dream, it was dusk, and Atticus could feel the darkness approaching. The air was thick with a yellow haze that nearly enveloped him and blocked out the rays of the sun, making the heat less oppressive.

He was standing naked and alone in the middle of a vast arena — at least he thought it was an arena. He couldn't see well enough to tell for sure. But he sensed that something was out there, just beyond the yellow haze. People, hundreds, maybe thousands. He could feel their presence.

Periodically the haze would thin. Then he would see, or think he saw, waving white handkerchiefs. He wondered if they were waving at him and, if they were, why. Were they trying to warn him of something? And if so, what?

There was a sound in the distance. Loud enough to distinguish it from silence but too far away for him to identify its nature. Sometimes, when the wind shifted, the sound became more distinct. It wasn't one sound, it was many sounds. The clash of steel on steel. A trumpet announcing he didn't know what. And there was more, even fainter, but still there. He could hear it if he stood perfectly still: wild animals, roaring mightily, somewhere in the haze.

The sounds frightened Atticus. He wanted to clasp his hands hard over his ears, shutting them out and putting an end to the frightening feeling. He hesitated, afraid to make a sudden move.

There were smells, too. The air was rancid and yet perfumed. He could smell the animals. He could smell their terror. He had smelled it before, hunting with his father. But this was different. This was the smell of animals that were trapped, caged, pacing, near panic.

There was another, even more terrifying smell fouling the air. A smell he had never encountered. A smell darker and more threatening than animal terror.

Were his ears playing tricks on him? At times the animals seemed to be out there, in the distance. At other times he thought he could hear them and feel them beneath him, underground, just below his feet. He could feel the earth shaking and rumbling, as if it were about to heave up and split, revealing an abyss into which he would fall and be lost forever.

LIKE THE GODS
ANNOUNCING THE END
OF TIME

❖ ◆ ❖ ◆ ❖

It was always at this point, never before and never after, that Atticus would awake, drenched in a cold sweat. It took him a while to realize where he was and even longer to remember how he came to be there.

Images flashed inside his head, appearing and evaporating:

His village, peaceful in the early morning hours.

His neighbors, like Atticus and his family, either half asleep or just beginning to stir about.

There had been no warning that day.

The Roman soldiers had vanquished the sentries guarding the village and easily overcome the fortifications that had taken so long to construct. Fortifications in which the villagers had fruitlessly put their faith.

Now there was no time. No time to think. No time to act.

The cavalry was already upon them, riding at full gallop, their swords drawn from their scabbards and glistening in the first rays of dawn, their horses' hooves pounding the ground like the gods announcing the end of time.

The infantry, wave upon wave of them: more than the grass that covered the ground or the sand on the beach. More men than Atticus had ever seen in his life converged on their defenseless town. Hundreds, maybe thousands, it was impossible to say. They were everywhere at once, impervious, protected by their huge shields and brass helmets. Slaughtering the frantic villagers while they slept or made futile attempts at escape.

And there was no time to say good-bye.

Before he knew it his father had pulled him from their hut, which had been struck by one of the flaming arrows, launched by unseen archers, falling on the village like a hailstorm from hell. But his mother and sister were still in there, trapped, their screams muffled by the crackling of the flames.

There was no time for comprehension, no time for grieving. Only moments later he and his father, along with a handful of other survivors, were being shackled, chained and dragged into captivity, their lives shattered and lost.

Three days later Atticus was separated from his father and sold to a slave trader. Tears flowed now, blurring his vision as he struggled to retain one last image of his beloved father, forced to stand powerless and mute as his son was taken from him.

Sparing Neither Expense nor Time

❖ ◆ ❖ ◆ ❖

Atticus remembered little other than the gash over his right eye and the fever that raged, it seemed, forever, burning his body and preventing his mind from functioning. He wanted to sleep during the day and was unable to at night.

He didn't even remember the morning he was bought by his new master. Not the slave market, the crowd or the auction.

Lucius Opimius was, at 1,500 denarii, the high bidder. He immediately directed Cassius Macedo, his personal physician, to nurse his new purchase back to health, "sparing neither expense nor time."

Cassius Macedo called for the following to be administered under his direction:

Opium

Anise

Coriander

Greek birthwort

The ash of five baked, wild swallow chicks, ground up and mixed with skimmed Attic honey

Cassius Macedo followed Lucius Opimius's instructions to the letter, caring for the patient personally during the day and making sure he was never left alone at night.

When Atticus's fever finally subsided enough for him to wonder where he was, the talkative physician answered many of the questions he dared not ask, lessening the weighty burden of complete confusion that enveloped him. Cassius Macedo told how Atticus came to be in Rome, explained much of his new and startling surroundings and, most important (and at great length), spoke to him about his new master.

TRUE ALLEGIANCE

❖ ◆ ❖ ◆ ❖

Lucius Opimius was a wealthy and respected member of the Roman aristocracy. His father and his father before him had been senators.

Ambitious and precocious, by the time he was twenty Lucius had a justly deserved reputation as one of the great advocates of his day.

In his most famous case he successfully defended two boys who were accused of poisoning their father. Their father had been a universally despised money lender. Lucius, to much acclaim, saved them both from suffering the traditional sentence for paracide: being sewn up in a sack with a dog, a cock, a viper and an ape and thrown into the depths of the sea.

The only case he lost, which resulted in the guilty

forger having his hands cut off, was considered a noble effort and a just verdict.

His rhetorical skills were legendary. People came from far and wide to hear him speak on any subject. His voice was soothing and pleasant, deceptively so, as if what he was saying wasn't all that important. As if it were something so simple that the listener himself might have come to the same conclusion, only hadn't found the time or words to express it. Knowing his voice was easy to listen to, perhaps too easy, he varied the pitch and tone just enough to ensure that his listeners didn't become so comfortable as to be complacent, and therefore uncomprehending.

He frowned on the extravagant gestures and rhetorical theatrics favored by his more flamboyant peers. He moved little while speaking, perhaps raising his left hand from time to time to emphasize a particularly important point. Or unexpectedly strolling away from the podium as if he had just remembered a previous, more important engagement, returning only when he felt he once again had his audience's full attention.

He was widely admired for his ethical and honorable conduct, something that distinguished him from nearly everyone around him in these times of pervasive greed and unethical and corrupt be-havior.

His influence was felt in all areas of Roman life: political, cultural and financial. There was no one in Rome he didn't know and no one who didn't know him.

It was even rumored that he had the Emperor's ear, the two having been boyhood friends. And, even further, that the Emperor never made an important decision without consulting him.

There was much talk of his political future: perhaps as a senator, like his father and grandfather, or, perhaps, even consul.

Then, quite unexpectedly, when he was only in his early thirties, Lucius Opimius precipitously retired from public life. He had, it appeared, consulted no one and never revealed the reason for his decision: a reason that had to remain known only to him and one other person.

The truth was, Lucius Opimius and the Emperor had been not simply boyhood friends, but true, best friends. Their closeness was bound not only by the veneer of the interests they shared — athletics, oratory, politics — but a deeper and more enduring emotional bond. The Emperor admired Lucius's unflappable and steadfast nature, and Lucius coveted, without jealousy, his friend's flair, charisma and vision.

Early in his reign the Emperor asked Lucius to make a secret sacrifice. The Emperor rightly believed that Rome was seething with intrigue and that his enemies lurked around every corner. Now that he was Emperor he would lose touch, there was no doubt about that. He would never be able to *really* know what was going on.

Lucius agreed, in effect, to go underground. To become the Emperor's eyes and ears, making it his business to know everyone and everything. Making it his sacred duty to protect his Emperor from all harm.

To all of Rome, Lucius's retirement was an unfathomable mystery, but to the Emperor it was the most precious of gifts — true allegiance.

The Loyal and Steadfast Nature that Lies Within

❖ ◆ ❖ ◆ ❖

Cassius Macedo was much concerned with matters of money, especially Lucius Opimius's money. He obsessed about the state of his will, even though Lucius was still a relatively young man. One never knew, however. And, as everyone did know, Lucius Opimius had no children and hence no heirs. Cassius hoped he would be remembered fondly in his will. In the meantime he was eager that Lucius not spend his money unwisely.

He was so agitated about Atticus that he mentioned to him numerous times that, at 1,500 denarii, Lucius Opimius had paid an exorbitant price for him. Cassius explained to a completely uncomprehending Atticus that the recent glut on the slave market — caused by the large number of successful campaigns waged by the invincible Roman legions — meant that each day prices were falling.

As far as Cassius was concerned 1,500 denarii was too much by half, especially considering the bigger, stronger and healthier boys that were available for much less. And, even more to Cassius's liking, the abundance of extraordinarily pretty, young girls who could be had for even less than that.

The decision baffled Cassius Macedo. Usually Lucius Opimius was so discerning when it came to purchasing slaves. Generally he preferred Greeks, whom he considered more intelligent and eager to learn than others. This boy was clearly from the northern provinces, not Greece. So the reason for this recent, impulsive purchase completely eluded Cassius.

He had accompanied Lucius Opimius to the auction that morning, never missing an opportunity to attend a slave auction.

Lucius Opimius had asked, more aloud and to himself than to his companion, whether he didn't see the intelligent look in the Roman boy's eyes and the sweet, sweet face. Cassius, who saw only a badly battered and bruised, scrawny boy from the provinces, could see no profit in disagreeing with Lucius. He said that there was indeed something special in the boy's face.

And didn't he see the loyal and steadfast nature that surely lay within? Master Lucius asked aloud. Frankly, Cassius Macedo did not see "the loyal and steadfast nature" that his master claimed "lay within" the boy. But the loyal and self-serving physician had, he believed, learned a great deal about human nature after all these years diagnosing illnesses. And what he learned was that all men liked to have what they thought confirmed by others, truth or falsehood being entirely irrelevant. And so he replied that he most assuredly did see it.

Of course Lucius Opimius's real motivation was too deep and too profound for Cassius Macedo's superficial nature. Lucius Opimius had come to the auction with the previous day's highly secret discussion with the Emperor still reverberating in his mind. He had never heard the Emperor so alarmed. Even the words he used were extreme and forbidding: *grave, crises, salvation, survival.*

Lucius was a serious man, used to serious dealings, but this mission called for something special. He would know it when he saw it, and when he saw Atticus he knew. The keen look in his eye, despite the pain. The tilt of his head, as if defying the cruel fate the gods had tossed his way. His youth. His innocence. Just what Lucius needed.

But the Emperor wasn't the only thing that concerned Lucius that morning at the slave auction. Haunting him was the still unbearable sadness caused by the recent death in childbirth of his wife.

Theirs had been that rarest of marriages: a peaceful, loving and harmonious relationship. They were rarely separated, never argued and had no secrets. They had been engaged to each other since they were infants.

She played the chithara for him, read her poems aloud (although they both knew he didn't care for poetry) and went to all the best plays (although he enjoyed discussing them with her later more than seeing them).

Lucius Opimius had been deeply in love with his wife, something he didn't fully realize until she was gone. And when she was gone he mourned her loss deeply.

But perhaps even more, or in a different way, he mourned the loss of the infant boy she was carrying. The son he longed for. The son who died along with the mother he never saw.

An Uncanny Likeness
of the Real Thing

❖　◆　❖　◆　❖

When Atticus fully recovered from his fever, he hoped that the dream would be gone, too. Much to his disappointment, although the fever was no more, the dream remained to haunt his nights.

During the day he tried to make sense of his new life. He was overwhelmed by the beauty and splendor he saw around him.

Lucius Opimius's twenty-two-room house was on the Palatine Hill, near the Emperor's residence. Although it was not the biggest or the most expensive house in that fashionable part of town, it offered a magnificent view of the city and was considered the most elegant, distinctive and tastefully appointed house on the Palatine.

Atticus had never seen anything that spacious and luxurious. He looked at the fountain in the court-yard and the heated marble seats in the latrine and wondered if he had been taken not to Rome but to a far-off land.

His physical surroundings, although strange and new, were at least a pleasure to behold. Not so the rest of his existence. His fever and the delirium that came with it had protected him till now.

Lucius Opimius had made it clear to his physi-cian that his new slave was to be treated differently than the others. And the good doctor dutifully communicated this to everyone in the household. The result now became all too clear to Atticus: The favoritism shown him by his new master provoked jealousy in the other slaves, who, without exception, shunned him.

A calm, easygoing boy from birth he never, ac-cording to his mother, cried or made a fuss. He followed the same pattern now, showing no emotion despite the hostility that surrounded him.

His unruffled appearance, however, was just that. An appearance, an impenetrable veneer that pro-tected him from the cruel realities of the outside world. It was like a mask, really, that he hid behind, now more than ever. A mask that was an uncanny likeness of the real thing.

Even if his usually perceptive new master, preoccupied as he was with a thousand and one things, had directed a more penetrating gaze his way, he would not have seen what lay behind the mask. He would not have seen the searing, unceasing pain caused by Atticus being forced to witness his mother's and sister's death at the hands of the callous and brutal Roman soldiers. He would not have seen the irreversible damage caused by his subsequent separation from his father. He would not see Atticus struggling now to endure the isolation and loneliness that had been added to his already inhuman burden.

THE TRUTH

The truth was that Atticus, who didn't suffer unduly from the affliction of modesty, believed that he fully deserved his favored treatment and looked down on the other slaves.

The only one who interested him in the slightest was the door slave, and that was only because of the whistle. The door slave, a boy his own age, guarded the door at night with a fierce-looking black-and-tan dog that was nearly as big as he was. The whistle was to be used in case of intruders.

Atticus had never seen a whistle before and dearly wanted to blow on it. But the door slave refused, like all the others, to acknowledge Atticus's existence in any way.

The truth is almost always more complicated and less lofty than it seems. And the truth was that if Atticus had had his choice, he would have willingly accepted the sidelong glances and the wall of silence in return for being excused, as he was, from the dreary and dreadful chores that were the sunup-to-sundown lot of the other three hundred slaves.

It all began at dawn, when the bell rang and the house slaves and domestic staff assembled to be assigned their daily duties: making the beds, cleaning and polishing the eating utensils and drinking goblets, emptying the charcoal from the braziers that heated the houses, lighting the oil lamps, carrying the litters, emptying the chamber pots on the upper floors and cleaning the lavatories and sponges on sticks that were used on the ground-floor.

And, perhaps, the most important chore of all: making sure there were no spiderwebs to be seen. Spiderwebs were the only things that frightened Lady Claudia, Lucius Opimius's recent young bride. She was so terrified of spiders that if, after inspecting the house, she discovered a web, even if it were of the most recent construction, the punishment could be most severe.

So every morning a band of house slaves dispersed, holding aloft long poles with cloths attached, seeking and destroying any spiderwebs lurking in even the farthest and remotest corners of the most little-used rooms in the house.

A Splendid Affair

❖ ◆ ❖ ◆ ❖

The young bride, who at fifteen was just three years above the minimum legal age, was initially purchased to be one of Lucius Opimius's household slaves, in fact, earlier at the very same auction as Atticus. At the wedding she wore a beautiful, full-length, white tunic and a bright orange veil over her elaborately constructed, ribboned hair. As was customary she wore her engagement ring on the second finger of her left hand, where it was thought to be connected, by a special nerve, directly to her heart.

After a pig was sacrificed, the witnesses were assembled and the marriage contract was signed.

Before vows were exchanged, the bride and her mother (who had been bought along with her

daughter and was given her freedom upon announcement of the engagement) pretended, as was
also the custom, that the bride had changed her
mind and needed to be torn away from her mother's loving but possessive embrace.

The procession to Lucius Opimius's home was
led by torch-bearing slaves and flute players, while
the line of guests followed behind singing merrily.

The bridegroom lifted his bride across the
threshold, and everyone took their seats for the
wedding feast, which lasted well into the night.

Lucius Opimius's decision to remarry, only four
months after the deaths of his wife and child, was
made without first consulting Aristide, his trusted
Greek astrologer. Aristide was troubled by the news.
Not because of any false sense of pride — he had rid
himself of that burden years earlier — but because
he knew his master's horoscope as well as he knew
his own. And he knew that recent transits of Saturn
and Jupiter indicated clearly that a "time of trial"
was about to present itself. According to the stars,
Lucius would need all those who claimed to be close
to him to prove their loyalty. This new addition was
not a complete surprise to Aristide. The planets
had pointed to some "unforeseen circumstances,"

but Aristide had mistakenly interpreted that to mean events, not people. Certainly, he concluded cautiously his master's bride-to-be was at best an unknown quantity.

Others were not as charitable as the worldly, wise astrologer. The decision astonished and displeased almost everyone close to Lucius Opimius. They could not help but compare Lady Claudia unfavorably to his first wife.

Lady Claudia had a plain face (a judgment some thought too kind); dressed extravagantly (his first wife had dressed elegantly but simply); doused herself with the most expensive Asiatic perfume; and tyrannized her hairdresser, masseuse, and manicurist, who all hovered near her constantly, fearing that they would not be within hearing distance when needed by their demanding mistress.

All were in agreement that she danced better than she should and that her preference for a good time over all else (resulting in her coming home at all hours of the night, sometimes with rumpled hair) was a scandal.

Predictably there were rumors about the reason for their betrothal. Lady Claudia, it was said, was able to obtain (from her scheming mother) a love potion that made her irresistible to Lucius Opimius.

Most considered her shallow and slow-witted.

A list of her positive qualities was painfully brief: youth and a rather ample chest.

But it was no love potion that made Lady Claudia irresistible to Lucius; it was the two things she promised. Her fertility promised him the son he longed for and her age the youth that was slipping through his fingers like fine sand.

Atticus was most curious about the eccentric astrologer. Unlike the others in the household (including Cassius Macedo and Lady Claudia) Aristide did not shun him. Unlike the others he did not appear to be threatened by the favoritism Lucius bestowed upon him.

But Aristide was rarely seen. He spent most of his time tinkering in his room and never went out unless he absolutely had to. The few times he and Atticus were in the same room there were always many people around, and besides, Atticus was too shy to do anything other than steal an occasional glance.

The astrologer was keeping a watchful eye on his master's carefully and purposefully chosen slave. Aristide wasn't sure of the specific purpose, but he knew there was one. Of course Atticus was not aware of being observed, because Aristide was too sly to allow him to have any inkling.

A Little Less Style
and a Little
More Substance

❖ ◆ ❖ ◆ ❖

As much as Atticus disliked the lowly, ordinary chores assigned to the other slaves, he felt quite the opposite about his own daily duties.

He awoke each day eager to begin, waiting outside Master Lucius's bedroom until he could hear him reading aloud to himself, which he did every morning to take advantage of the light. This was a sign that it was safe for Atticus to enter. He could then proceed with his first task, although one could hardly call it that.

He sat and listened silently while his master chafed at the "intolerable burden" of having to wear a toga. Atticus would listen while his master cried out how he already couldn't wait to return home from the day's activities so he could shed it.

Master Lucius was quite stoic in most matters, but this was his only area of constant complaint.

Atticus had to admit that he did have a point. It required a great deal of skill to artfully drape the elaborate garment over the body so that the folds fell properly. Even with the help of his able valet it was a tedious and time-consuming job.

"Sheer idiocy" was the way Master Lucius put it, pointing out that only something as frivolous as fashion would require someone to wear a garment that wasn't warm enough in winter and was too hot in the summer.

"Today everyone dresses above their means. We Romans could do with a little less style and a little more substance."

Impractical as it might be, Atticus noted that his master, like all other Roman men, never went anywhere without it.

Once the morning ritual was over, Lucius Opimius gathered his toga together and threw it over his shoulder with a sweeping gesture that signaled that — once Atticus put on his sandals for him — they were ready to greet his patient and loyal clients.

THE CONTINUED
BENEVOLENCE OF THEIR
MOST HONORED PATRON

❖ ◆ ❖ ◆ ❖

Each day, there were hundreds of clients to be dealt with, an accurate daily gauge of Lucius Opimius's continued reputation as a wise and just patron.

They had been there since the first crowing of the cock, lining up outside his front door (the earliest arrivals kicking on the door to announce their presence). They gathered daily to express their most humble and grateful appreciation for the continued benevolence of their most honored patron.

Unlike his peers, who employed a long list of excuses — too busy, too sick, out of town — Lucius Opimius never turned anyone away, taking as much time as necessary to listen to every client's case, regardless of merit or magnitude.

Writers, poets and philosophers were also known to gather outside the house on Palatine Hill on any given morning. They hoped to exchange one of their stories, rhymes or profound insights in return for Lucius Opimius simply looking upon them favorably, shining his light their way, like a torch in the night.

Many used flattery to advance their cause, describing for their patron the temples they had visited recently to place curses on his enemies, and the statues and monuments they were planning to erect in his honor.

Lucius Opimius did not allow himself to be flattered by compliments like this. Early on he remarked to Atticus, who was surprised more by his master's candor than his cynicism, that they were interested only in what they could get from him.

Some weren't satisfied with simply greeting him and offering up their pleas. They requested, begged even, to accompany him on his daily rounds, wherever his business might take him that day, pointing out (erroneously) how much help they would be.

Atticus took great pride in knowing that his master insisted that only Atticus accompany him on his daily rounds.

After all the clients were properly greeted, the two returned to Master Lucius's bedchamber, where he hastily ate breakfast: bread dunked in wine with cheese and honey, or sometimes fruit alone. Atticus handed him a clear jar of water, which he splashed on his face and poured into his mouth to rinse his teeth and gums.

Soon, they were off to conduct the day's business.

A Foul Odor That Never Quite Went Away

❖ ◆ ❖ ◆ ❖

His master, Atticus soon learned, was not someone who liked to tarry on life's path. He preferred, at all times, to move at a decisive pace.

He rarely rode in his litter, preferring the invigorating exercise of a brisk walk. Atticus tried to keep up with his long-legged, athletic master, but his short legs would carry him only so fast; he often lagged behind. It was all Atticus could do not to lose sight of his master as he effortlessly wove his way through the narrow, twisted, crowded streets.

It was nearly impossible to walk down some of the streets, so crowded were they with people shopping in the small shops that sold everything from fish to fruit.

Traveling performers — jugglers, fortune-tellers,

snake charmers — took up even more space, entertaining the crowd in hopes of picking up some spare change.

Atticus was astounded that so many people were able to fit into one city, even a city as big as Rome. People lived in incredibly high apartment buildings (some five stories), so high that they cast shadows on the streets below. People lived one right on top of the other, some in dark basement hovels that were buried in underground cellars. Garbage lay rotting in the streets, and combined with the contents of chamber pots, it created a foul odor that never quite went away.

Virtually Invisible

❖ ◆ ❖ ◆ ❖

Atticus was always relieved when he made it to their usual first stop, the barbershop.

Like many of Rome's wealthy citizens, Lucius Opimius could have one of his slaves cut his hair and give him a shave every morning. But Lucius enjoyed the informal social nature of the barbershop too much. It was an opportunity for him to keep his ear to the ground, especially now.

Though he was without vanity in matters of the mind and the spirit, Lucius made up for it when it came to his body.

He lectured Atticus on all aspects of personal hygiene, especially the importance of greeting the world each day with a freshly shaven face. A man with an unshaven face, Lucius warned, looks and kisses like a he-goat.

He was most diligent about maintaining his appearance, especially after turning forty this past year. He was always particular about how his hair was cut, but now that it was no longer strictly ebony (he laughed when Atticus told him he thought his gray hair made him look more distinguished, saying he didn't want to look more distinguished), he was even more particular. Truth was, it was the thinning more than the grayness that disturbed him. It was a situation that Lucius Opimius looked upon with the utmost gravity.

When Atticus first accompanied his master to the barbershop, he sat on the bench that lined the wall opposite the one where the mirrors were hung so the customers could keep an eye on things while their hair was cut.

People continued their conversations, no matter how intimate, as if he were deaf or simply not there. Because he was a young slave they assumed he was too stupid to understand what they were talking about — although what they were talking about wasn't difficult to understand.

Atticus had already discovered that, as a young slave, he was virtually invisible, especially to Roman citizens of wealth and power. In fact, the greater the wealth and power, the greater his powers of invisibility.

Atticus, who was quite curious by nature, was delighted with his discovery.

His barber, according to Master Lucius, was most adroit at applying the hot towel the necessary amount of time to achieve the crucial moisture level necessary for a smooth shave. He also knew how to properly care for and sharpen his razor. Master Lucius could not tolerate nicks and cuts marring his face. His barber was also without equal when it came to applying the soothing unguents and giving the most invigorating scalp massage.

After a few visits, Atticus began playing with two children who belonged to one of the barbers. The boy was his age, although much bigger, since Atticus was small for his age.

While his baby sister played with her rag doll, the two boys played with marbles, rode a hobbyhorse, used bricks to erect buildings that were so high they leaned too far one way or the other and came crashing down just like real ones, and played with the boy's pet mouse, which he had trained to pull a miniature carriage around the shop.

The most fun, however, was playing gladiator. The boy taught Atticus how, choosing himself to be a *retiarius* and pretending he had a net and a long trident, while Atticus was a *bestiarius,* a gladiator who fought wild animals with only a knife.

A Fate That Was
not for Him

❖ ◆ ❖ ◆ ❖

After the barbershop Lucius Opimius
embarked on a constant round of quiet conversations with a wide variety of people on an even wider
variety of topics: business, politics, foreign affairs,
finances, art, culture, entertainment and personal
matters. Master Lucius's appointments took them
to every part of the city.

The next and last stop before the market was the
baths. The baths were in the largest building Atticus
had ever seen. It covered several city blocks.

Here Lucius Opimius could meet with the consuls, senators, magistrates, lawyers, politicians and
businessmen who ran the city of Rome.

As soon as he arrived, Lucius exchanged his toga
for one of the linen sheets the attendants in the

cloakroom kept on hand especially for him. There were casual hellos and informal inquiries about health and family. Then more quiet, discrete conversations, one-on-one or in small groups. Atticus found it remarkable that his master was able to carry on a conversation with all the whistling, singing and shouting back and forth that went on in the cavernous rooms.

After an appropriate time Lucius Opimius excused himself to exercise, something he did nearly every day. He rarely allowed business matters to intrude on his rigid regimen. He was horrified as he watched his contemporaries, previously lean young men, slowly but inevitably turning into fat, middle-aged men right before his eyes. It was a fate that was not for him. He carefully watched what he ate; drank wine in moderation, if at all; fasted occasionally; ate no foods that contained acids; and used emetics and purgatives frequently.

When the water was warm enough he swam in the Tiber River once a week. The rest of the time he worked out at the baths: lifting weights, tossing the medicine ball, fencing and boxing.

After working up a good sweat, enough so that the impurities in his body were released, he had the dirt and grime scraped away by a slave with a strigil. Now, at last, it was time for his reward: a massage.

While Atticus stood by, in case his master required anything, Lucius closed his eyes and succumbed to the kneading, knowing fingers of the masseuse, who poured scented oil from a little pitcher she kept by her side onto Lucius's dark-skinned, muscular body. It was the only time Lucius Opimius truly relaxed. As she worked her magic Master Lucius purred like a kitten.

As a final touch Lucius, who could not tolerate any body hair on his person whatsoever, had his daily appointment with one of the expert depilators. She investigated every pore of his body to make sure there were no newly emergent hairs just surfacing, and if there were, she removed them forthwith.

Afterward, at the clubhouse, he stretched out on the mats, rising only occasionally to walk carefully (for it was easy to slip on the slick, wet marble floors) to the warm pool. Even though his own physician recommended it for a number of ailments, he couldn't bring himself to plunge into the cold pool. Then it was off to the steam room, where the most lengthy conversations took place.

Although Lucius was rarely alone in the baths (or

anywhere else for that matter) he savored those few moments when he was. Solitude was a rare and precious commodity to him and he wasted none of it.

He strolled aimlessly through the garden promenade, letting his thoughts wander, a luxury he hardly indulged in anymore. He browsed through some of the books in the well-stocked library, silently admonishing himself for not reading as much as he should (certainly not as much as Aristide, his learned Greek astrologer). He idly watched the various groups deep in conversation, delighted, for once, to not be participating. He declined repeatedly and without exception all the food offered by the various vendors who came around incessantly, hawking their wares.

Sometimes, however, Lucius spent so much time at the baths that they hardly had time to get to market and shop for dinner.

THIS MOST
DELICATE MATTER

❖ ◆ ❖ ◆ ❖

One morning, after Atticus had been in Lucius Opimius's service for a year, his master spoke to him about a mission that required cunning, concentration and the utmost discretion. He could say nothing about it to anyone.

These past months Atticus had come to learn how much his master cared for him. The other slaves slept, helter-skelter, all over the house, but Master Lucius insisted that Atticus sleep down the corridor from his bedroom, so as not to be too far away.

Even when Master Lucius was ill and confined to bed, which was rare, he requested that Atticus remain by his side.

Lucius Opimius believed he could trust Atticus

from that first day he saw him at the slave auction, and he believed it now. Atticus glowed in the light cast upon him by his master's trust. But as much as he was flattered, he was also frightened.

He knew his master was a good and true man; perhaps as good and true as any Roman could be. But Atticus was no fool. He knew the conversations his master had each day involved behind-the-scenes maneuvers that were as dangerous as they were clandestine.

Now Master Lucius proceeded to explain what he called "this most delicate matter."

This particular morning Lucius would not be going to the barbershop. Atticus would go alone. Shortly after he arrived, a man accompanied by his entourage would enter the barbershop. Master Lucius described the man in great detail, as he wanted there to be no mistake as to which one was the object of their attention.

He was to remain close to the man, whose name was Galerius Traculus, the entire time he was in the barbershop, no matter where he went. Close enough to hear any conversation he had, but not so close that he was noticed and therefore aroused suspicion.

Master Lucius was counting on Atticus's flawless

memory, a characteristic he had taken note of early on. Atticus must remember everything, no matter how trivial and unimportant it might sound to him.

Everything Lucius Opimius repeated, his sky-blue eyes unblinking. Atticus had never seen his master look so solemn. He nodded, and that, combined with the intense look on his face, was the sign his master required.

THE ODOR HUNG ABOUT HIM LIKE A STORM CLOUD

❖ ◆ ❖ ◆ ❖

Lucius Opimius's description of Galerius Traculus was accurate down to the finest detail. When he had first described their quarry Atticus thought that surely he was exaggerating. But as soon as the man walked in, barking out orders to his bowing and scraping retinue, just as his master said he would, Atticus realized that if anything, his master was being diplomatic.

Galerius Traculus did in fact comb his few remaining strands of hair from one side to the other in a futile attempt to cover his bald and shiny dome. And he did wear so much perfume that the odor hung about him like a storm cloud. His face, as described, was made up like a woman's; his cheeks rouged to camouflage his unfortunate complexion, obviously the result of some ravenous skin disease.

But his most outstanding characteristic, and the one that convinced Atticus that this was his man, was his weight. He was the fattest man Atticus had ever seen, and his stomach protruded so far out that even his billowy toga couldn't hide it.

Thus assured, Atticus proceeded as instructed. Galerius Traculus had, within minutes of entering, engaged in an intense conversation with a nervous man who had been anxiously waiting his arrival. Atticus had noticed him because by now he had grown familiar with nearly all the patrons. This man he had never seen there before.

The man was agitated the entire time they spoke. Atticus could hear it in his voice and could tell by the way he kept looking around to see if anyone was watching them, ignoring the one person who was.

Emboldened by his cloak of invisibility Atticus sat right next to the two of them on the bench, where he could hear every word.

His assignment became problematic only when Galerius Traculus was being shaved. Atticus improvised, playing gladiator with the son of one of the barbers so he could run around the barber chair at will and be close enough to hear.

His most difficult decision came when the two men went into the latrine. Surely, Atticus thought, if he followed them there he would be noticed. He decided to risk it, and his boldness paid off. He sat there in the latrine, opposite them, while they continued as if he wasn't there.

Bought and Paid For

❖ ◆ ❖ ◆ ❖

Master and slave met a few streets distant from the barbershop, as planned.

Atticus recounted in perfect detail the conversations he overheard: the trivial along with the substantive.

Galerius Traculus had done most of the talking: He spoke of his stable of beautiful, white Arabian horses — the price of good breeding stock being at least five times that of a slave; his growing collection of gems and fine vases; his aviary filled with chattering parrots; a special carriage he was having fitted with a gaming board for dice; the gold cosmetic box and duck earrings from Syria he had bought for his wife; whether it was true that lamp soot could help keep your hair black; a painful visit from the dentist who had pulled a tooth that very morning; his health, which was deteriorating because his epileptic fits were becoming more frequent; whether or not eight baths a day was softening his muscles; and that just as soon as he left the barbershop he was going to get a piping hot sausage from the street vendor right outside.

But he spent most of his time on more serious matters.

He talked about a dear friend who had died tragically. He had thrown a pear up in the air and was amusing his dinner guests, who had bet that he couldn't catch it in his mouth, when it stuck in his throat and he suffocated.

He bragged about his recent trial that everyone in Rome was talking about. There were so many spectators that they had to set up temporary stands to accommodate everyone. All that trouble, he complained, just because one of his buildings had collapsed. The nerve of the victims relatives accusing him of using inferior materials in order to pocket extra money. As if it was his fault so many people got killed.

He laughed and said that the verdict was never in doubt because two of the jurors had been bought and paid for.

He told his companion about the enormous amount of money — 800 million sesterces — he was spending on the upcoming games he was sponsoring. And how pleased he was that the Emperor, although not exactly approving of his plans, had done nothing to stop them from going forward.

He talked about the chariot races, the nautical battle, the wild animals he was having hunted down, trapped and brought from all over the world back to Rome and the gladiatorial combat. He was going to have an unprecedented three hundred pairs of animals fighting — all decked out in silver armor. It was going to be entertainment more glorious than any seen before in the history of Rome. He hoped it would keep the mob amused and diverted, at least until things settled down.

But it was the conversation in the latrine that was the longest and most serious sounding. It made Atticus doubly glad he had ventured forth.

It was about what Galerius Traculus viewed as the sorry state of Rome: the current grain shortage; the pirates who had, once again, intercepted a Roman ship, this time with women aboard. The quality of life had deteriorated; you dared not venture out at night without having made up your will first. He had to take seven slaves with him — two to light the way with torches and the rest to protect him from the hoodlums who had nothing better to do than roam the streets, vandalize shops and intimidate respectable citizens like him. He didn't allow his wife to go anywhere without an escort.

If the Emperor didn't do something about the situation soon, someone else would have to.

A Man
Without Qualities

❖ ◆ ❖ ◆ ❖

Lucius Opimius told Atticus that the less he knew about Galerius Traculus the better off he would be. But curious Atticus could not leave it at that.

In the following days and weeks he kept his ears especially attuned to dinner conversations, idle chatter among the clients in the morning and most fruitful, discussions overheard in the barbershop and the baths. It wasn't long before he was able to piece together a full picture of the person his master privately called a man without qualities.

Rich, powerful, dishonest and *corrupt* were the words most frequently used to describe Galerius Traculus.

Estimates as to the extent of his vast fortune

varied wildly, but all agreed that it had been built, literally, on the misfortunes of others.

Galerius Traculus was a real estate developer who had his finger in every construction pie. He directed his underlings to buy up apartment houses that had been damaged by one of the numerous fires that plagued the city of Rome. He then rebuilt them using the cheapest materials and, to further maximize his profits, charged the new tenants the most inflated rate imaginable.

Most people were terrified of him. He had a well-deserved reputation for gratuitous cruelty. He had stabbed one of his slaves in the eye, blinding him with his pen, just because he thought the slave had looked at him funny. He kept a huge fish tank filled with giant, man-killing lampreys as a standing threat to any misbehaving slaves. All his slaves wore bands around their necks saying, "I have run away. If captured, return me to my master: Galerius Traculus, Rome." And if any of them had children, they were drowned like unwanted kittens.

His first wife had "fallen" five stories to her death. Galerius Traculus claimed he had been asleep at the time, that his wife had been ill and had committed suicide. There was, however, no medical record of any illness, and people who were with his wife that morning reported that she was in the best of spirits. He had inherited her rather large personal fortune.

It was said, however, that the only thing he truly lusted after and lacked was political power.

He Accepted with Great Delight

❖ ◆ ❖ ◆ ❖

When word spread throughout the household that Lucius Opimius was planning, just two weeks hence (which everyone agreed wasn't nearly enough time) one of his special dinners, the entire staff launched into an immediate frenzy of activity.

Master Lucius historically didn't decide the final menu until the absolute last minute, but an extensive preliminary list of potential ingredients was composed anyway:

Boar, venison, goat, mutton, hare, dormice, ostrich, duck, partridge, pigeon, pheasant, goose, capon, snails and foie gras.

Lobster, sea urchin, mullet and oysters.

Cheese, eggs, pickles, olives, mushrooms, celery, thyme, coriander, pepper, oregano and juniper berries.

An informal man in most respects and disapproving of the ostentation that was becoming more and more common each day, Master Lucius did not hold back when it came to one of his banquets.

The special dining room, which hadn't been touched since the wedding, was readied. The three couches that were normally there remained around the low dining room table, but additional ones were brought in. The silver and crystal drinking goblets were polished and the utensils and plates prepared.

Usually Lucius Opimius invited only a small number of people to dinner — often three, six at most. But this was different. The guest list, which still had not been finalized, included a number of senators, distinguished lawyers, writers and poets — nearly twenty people in all.

Lucius Opimius was known throughout Rome as a gracious host and a serious gourmet. He employed not one but two of the finest chefs in the land and a pastry chef who was without equal. All three were masters of their trade. They had often been tempted by generous offers from others. But they never succumbed, knowing that only Master Lucius truly appreciated their artistry.

Invitations to one of his feasts — and they were exactly that — were highly prized. Whereas other hosts concerned themselves with how many and how famous their guests were, Lucius concerned himself with the exotic nature of the succulent dishes being served.

Unlike many of Rome's hosts, Lucius frowned on the accepted practice of giving the better dishes to those one wished to impress and the inferior ones to the rest.

Although he was well aware that in Rome status was everything — who was invited, where they sat and what they ate and drank all had grave implications — he simply didn't care.

Nor did he care about the conventional wisdom when it came to serving wine. The good wine was usually served at the beginning of dinner and the not so good toward the end, when no one would be able to tell the difference.

Lucius Opimius insisted that the finest wines from all around the world be served throughout the meal.

Food and wine were not the only important decisions being made. There was entertainment and music to decide on.

Lucius rejected the usual fare: Spanish dancing girls, conjurers, acrobats.

And everyone knew there would be no singing. Singing interfered with conversation, and conversation was the reason Lucius Opimius gave a dinner party. Conversation and the information it could provide. If there was something Lucius wanted to know, some piece of a puzzle that was missing, a dinner party often provided what he was looking for.

Which was why, for the first time, Galerius Traculus had been invited. Although every bit as rich as Master Lucius and, in a cruder way, as powerful, Galerius Traculus didn't travel in the same circles that Lucius Opimius did.

The invitation surprised and pleased him. He looked upon it as a sign that he had finally arrived. He had known it all along but the invitation confirmed it. He was about to enter the top echelon of aristocratic Roman society.

Were he as cautious a man as he should have

been, Galerius Traculus would have looked upon the invitation with some skepticism. But vanity trumps reality, especially in Rome, and rather than be suspicious of the invitation, he accepted it with great delight.

Peacock Feathers Kept the Flies off the Food

❖ ◆ ❖ ◆ ❖

All three chefs attempted to outdo the others by coming up with the most outrageous dishes for Lucius Opimius's consideration. As expected, he made his final decision only days before the evening of the banquet:

- ◆ Fresh fruit: apples, pears and figs
- ◆ Dry and fresh dates
- ◆ Cream soup with minced lobster and chopped garlic
- ◆ Cold-pressed, smoked duck with grapes and oranges
- ◆ Dormice cooked in honey and poppy seeds
- ◆ Thrush's tongues in wild honey

- Sow's udder stuffed with fried baby mice
- Honeyed squab boned, stuffed with pine nuts and barley, baked slowly in brandy and fig syrup and served with tiny sausages made of chopped smoked lamb's tongue
- Boar garnished with truffles and mushrooms
- Cheese
- Honey and sweetened cakes
- Pastries
- Wines: Syprian, vintage flarian, Greek and home-made via Capua

The guest list had been reviewed with as much care and consideration as the menu. Lady Claudia deliberated even longer than her husband, making additions and deletions until the very last minute. In the end twenty-two people were selected, all of whom, of course, accepted.

The big night finally came, and as the distinguished guests arrived, the slaves took off their shoes, washed their feet and put slippers on them.

Each guest was announced by one of the slaves and shown to his particular couch and his particular place on the couch.

Lucius Opimius was quite formal when it came to the proper seating protocol for his banquets.

The most distinguished guests were placed nearest the host, who looked regal and relaxed in his brightly colored Greek robe. To his right sat the guest of honor, General Marius Maximus, who had just been awarded a triumph. The triumph was his reward for a most successful and lucrative campaign in the northern provinces.

Next to the General was Caius Curtius, recently elected senator for life, who wore the toga with the purple band signifying his membership in the senate.

Some of the guests arrived quite drunk, having spent the previous hours in the baths. One elderly gentleman was so sick he had to lie down and was not seen upright until the evening had ended and he was taken home by his wife and brother-in-law.

The dining room, which had been reviewed carefully by Lucius Opimius the night before, looked glittering and glorious. Every knife, spoon and toothpick was properly placed, and the couches were lined up precisely. At the very last minute Master Lucius had decided that the plates should be replaced with the ones that had the twelve signs of the zodiac on them.

The evening began easily.

Lucius Opimius entertained his guests with one of his favorite tricks: peeling the skin off an apple in one long, continuous piece, which he then held up and displayed, much to everyone's amusement.

There were animated conversations about a new book of poetry whose verses were considered both graceful and witty, and the latest play to open in Rome, everyone agreeing that they loved going to the theater. According to this gathering, the Theater of Pompei was putting on the most entertaining plays.

The skilled waiters brought out bowls of food, placed selected dishes on the individual tables and began to carve up the boar with hunting knives.

Some slaves handed out napkins so that guests could cover the couch, protecting it from stains. Some of course chose to fill the napkins with leftovers, which they took home. Other slaves circulated silently throughout the evening with bowls of perfumed water for the guests to wash their dirty, greasy fingers. Still others stood by with towels draped over their arms so the guests could dry their hands when ready. All assembled were fanned with peacock feathers that kept the flies off the food.

In between each course there was entertainment: first, a poet; and second, a jester who poked fun at some of the guests, although no one seemed to mind, either because of the good-natured atmosphere that prevailed or the fine wine that flowed ceaselessly.

FRIEND FOR LIFE

❖ ◆ ❖ ◆ ❖

But everyone agreed that by far the most imaginative and entertaining portion of the evening (and a tribute to Lucius's refusal to accept the ordinary) were the three actors who used mime and masks to tell their story, which was called "Androcles and the Lion."

It was a simple if far-fetched tale of a young slave named Androcles who, having escaped from a cruel master, hid in a cave. The cave, however, turned out to be inhabited by a lion. This particular lion had a problem: A rather large thorn was imbedded deep into the soft part of his bloodied and painfully swollen paw.

The normally ferocious beast was at his wits' end about his paw. He appealed to Androcles for help by moaning and groaning piteously and putting his paw heavily in the terrified slave's lap.

The good-natured Androcles willingly obliged, pulling the thorn from the lion's paw and creating a friend for life. They lived together happily for some time, the lion hunting for food each day.

One morning Androcles was captured by Roman soldiers, brought back to the village from which he had escaped and sentenced to death in the arena.

Who should be sent out to devour Androcles but the very same lion. Recognizing his savior he stroked his face with the now healed paw.

The Emperor, understandably intrigued by this and hearing from Androcles the reason for their mutual affection, freed the lion and the slave and returned both to their original habitats, where they lived happily ever after.

Not only was the unlikely story charming but the masks added an element that was most creative and inventive.

Androcles's mask showed him in various emotional states: oppressed by his master, terrified by the lion, woebegone when captured, resigned in the arena and joyous in the end.

The lion's masks were even better, portraying his agony, his gratitude and his fond recognition.

There's Truth in Wine

❖ ◆ ❖ ◆ ❖

Master Lucius's guests were having a good time gobbling down the delicious food, blowing their noses into their napkins and excusing themselves every few minutes to go vomit so that they could continue eating. The slaves had their hands full, running around cleaning off any guests who, unable or unwilling to leave, had thrown up on themselves.

The handpicked wines were poured through funnels and strainers into bowls, where they were diluted half and half with water and cooled off with snow brought in from the mountains. The bowls were then emptied into the guest's drinking goblets.

Atticus made certain he was the only one who served his master wine. Lucius Opimius wanted his wine diluted to a greater degree than the others.

"There's truth in wine, my son," Lucius confided. "People say the most extraordinary things when drunk, and I don't want to miss anything."

Galerius Traculus arrived quite drunk and immediately insisted that his wine be undiluted.

His wife, Tanusia, arrived separately, but equally drunk, and announced that her pet marmoset had died and that she was now the owner of what was unquestionably the smallest dwarf in the Roman world. Apparently there had been talk that someone in the northern provinces had a female that was even smaller, but at two feet, one palm, hers did indeed turn out to be the smallest. Owning dwarfs had become quite fashionable recently.

Not surprisingly, perhaps because of their similar young age, Lady Claudia and Tanusia got along famously. For one thing they had fashion in common. They discussed the origins of the silk dresses they both wore; Tanusia's emeralds and pearls; Lady Claudia's dolphin-shaped gold earrings, bronze ankle bracelet and elegant pendant, which hung from her neck needlessly calling attention to her cleavage.

They discussed lipsticks, makeup, powder boxes and their various phobias. Lady Claudia confessed most confidentially her fear of spiders, and Tanusia her inability to live in a house if there was a knot anywhere within it.

They whispered about General Maximus, who liked to show off his fierce-looking scars and who secretly kept a harem; Fulvia Dolabella, who was exiled to an unknown Libyan desert location, where she starved herself to death; and Scribonia Serapio, who was getting divorced because she claimed her husband was of bad moral character.

The discussion became most animated when they discovered their mutual admiration for, and attraction to, gladiators. They exchanged notes on their current favorites and important inside information. Lady Claudia suggested that the warm blood from a freshly killed gladiator would be most helpful in healing Galerius Traculus's epilepsy, and Tanusia offered that if Lady Claudia used a dead gladiator's spear to part her hair, it would bring her good luck.

The story of Androcles seemed to spur Galerius Traculus into a long discourse on the proper treatment of slaves — a discourse that went on while he continued devouring his two squabs, tearing them apart with his hands and ripping off each shred of meat with his blackened teeth, while the fat and grease dribbled down the front of his white toga.

He was lecturing Titus Flaminius, a highly respected financier. Flaminius was quite surprised to find Galerius Traculus among the guests at a dinner hosted by Lucius Opimius. He was an old and true friend and had been so to Lucius's father, and had come to trust him, without question. As inexplicable as Galerius Traculus's presence seemed, Titus Flaminius assumed that Lucius had his reasons. He received the unwanted lecturer with passive grace.

Titus Flaminius had a reputation for treating his slaves most kindly. It was well known that his will provided for the freeing of all his slaves upon his death. Recently he had freed a gravely ill longtime slave so that the slave could have his last wish and be buried a free man.

It was precisely behavior like this that was ruining today's slaves, according to Galerius Traculus. Slaves had to be whipped regularly, although always after being caned as a warning and never by the master's own hand. If they weren't they would steal you blind.

Abruptly leaving the topic of the proper handling of slaves without even pausing for breath, Galerius Traculus launched into an even longer and louder oration, jumping from topic to topic with little rhyme or reason.

The situation in Rome had gotten out of hand, he said. Someone had to bring order to the chaos. There were too many suspicious people lurking about — he had had to double his guard at night; anyone in Rome could be bought; that was how he had gotten where he was today; he knew all the right people; everybody had their price; once he set his mind to something, nothing could stop him; just wait until the games began.

The Art of Listening

❖ ◆ ❖ ◆ ❖

As instructed, Atticus, who had no other duties, attended to his master throughout the evening. This amounted to very little activity, and the slave boy watched his master closely. After the initial pleasantries and introductions had been dispensed with, the food served and the wine amphoras uncorked, Lucius had really said very little, content to recline on his couch and take it all in.

Master Lucius was the master of many things, not the least of which was the art of listening, an art of which most Romans were ignorant.

It would be impossible to see from the position of his body, for there was no tell-tale shifting forward at a particular moment, as if his interest had been piqued; no untoward turn of the head to indicate anything of note was being said; not even an un-guarded movement of the eyes indicating anything other than casual interest.

There was no way to tell that Lucius Opimius was focused completely on the behavior and conversation of Galerius Traculus.

Only Atticus saw that Lucius Opimius had found what he was looking for: one of the missing pieces of the puzzle. He had known the what, and now he had the when. All he needed to know was the who.

Having gotten the information he wanted, Master Lucius immediately lost interest in the banquet. The sheerest of veils fell over his eyes, removing him just slightly from what was going on around him.

He allowed the evening to conclude as Lady Claudia had planned. The dining room ceiling opened and tiny flasks of costly Capua perfumes were lowered on strings, one for each of the guests to take home as a memento.

Galerius Traculus's wife was delighted. She told Lady Claudia that it was an evening she would never forget.

The comment made Aristide, Lucius Opimius's learned Greek astrologer, smile. Comments like this always made Aristide smile. He positively hated these dinners, considered them boring beyond comprehension, but his presence was required at each and every dinner by Lucius, who valued his opinion too highly to do without it. Aristide attended in body but in spirit he was truly somewhere else.

Tanusia's remark made the evening worthwhile, for Aristide knew that she was right. It *was* an evening she would never forget.

When the last of the guests left, the slaves rushed in to clean up. The floor was littered with boar, duck and squab bones, lobster shells, date pits, orange peels, half-eaten apples, already rotting pears and melon husks.

THE MAN IN THE AISLE SEAT

❖ ◆ ❖ ◆ ❖

Two weeks after the banquet Master Lucius gave Atticus another assignment. It was, he said, more complicated than the previous one.

Atticus was to attend the chariot races the next day. He was to arrive early and sit in a specific seat in the upper tiers. Eventually Galerius Traculus would arrive, uncharacteristically unaccompanied.

He will sit three rows in front of Atticus and one seat from the aisle, Master Lucius said. After a while a man will come, look around quizzically, as if he isn't sure where he wants to sit and decide to take the seat next to Galerius Traculus.

Initially neither will greet the other. When Galerius Traculus feels certain that no one is watching, he will talk to the man in the aisle seat. The conversation will, in all likelihood, continue for some time, with Galerius Traculus doing all the talking. When it is concluded, the man will get up and leave the arena.

Shortly afterward there will be another man who will repeat the same, exact pattern. Over the course of the afternoon four men will do this.

Atticus's mission was to provide Master Lucius with a detailed physical description of all four men. The more accurate the description Atticus provided, the less chance there was for error. "A great deal is riding on this, my son," Master Lucius said, not to scare Atticus but to indicate how much confidence he had in him.

As directed, Atticus arrived quite early so as to be sure to get the seat he wanted. He watched as the people arrived, talking, eating, laughing and betting on their favorite teams. Galerius Traculus hadn't arrived yet, so Atticus was able to watch the leather-helmeted charioteers parade around the enormous track.

Thanks to the rather raucous conversation that was taking place right behind him, he learned that twenty-four races were scheduled for that day; that each race was seven laps; that there were mostly two-horse teams but one race would use four-horse teams. The people seated behind him were greatly disappointed that no ten-horse teams would be, as previously announced, racing that day. Almost everyone in his section was rooting for the green teams, some people wearing that color to show their support. Hardly anyone was cheering for the red, blue or white teams.

Galerius Traculus seemed to appear out of nowhere, alone, as Master Lucius said he would. He took the seat one removed from the aisle. Atticus kept one eye trained on the empty seat next to him and the other on the action on the track.

The first race was getting under way, but Atticus paid no attention. The chariot drivers, in their short tunics and bare arms covered in wild boar dung (the smell of it was said to prevent the horses from stomping them to death if they were thrown from their chariots) checked to make sure they had tucked their knives into their belts. That way, if there was an accident and they got tangled up in the reins, they could cut themselves free.

Atticus could hear, even all the way up where he was, the horses impatiently pawing the ground and snorting while all around him the crowd yelled for the white cloth signaling the start of the race to be dropped.

The chariots broke from the starting gate and began to thunder around the track. They were tightly packed, riding wheel to wheel, nearly colliding on every deadly turn. They tried to block each other, force their opponents to the outside, or hook their wheels and suddenly swerve away, hoping to separate a wheel from an axle, sending the chariot into oblivion.

By the time the first race was over, the first man had arrived and taken the vacant seat next to Galerius Traculus. Atticus immediately began making a mental list: height, weight, age, eye color, hair color, clothes, outstanding characteristics.

By the time the second man arrived, the sixth race was over. And by the time the last lap of the last race had been run, the last of the four men had arrived.

THE TRUTH CAN ALWAYS BE DISTINGUISHED FROM ALL ELSE

❖ ◆ ❖ ◆ ❖

Atticus, his mission accomplished, was eager to return to his master, but instinctively he sensed there was more to be done. Atticus rarely acted on instinct — life had taught him to be cautious and considerate, not brash and bold.

But this inner voice was insistent — he could not bring himself to go against it. He remained in his seat and kept an eye on Galerius Traculus.

It wasn't long before Galerius Traculus rose heavily from his seat, swirled the ample material of his toga around him and hurried up the stadium stairs.

Atticus quickly followed, lagging behind only as much as he had to, more fearful of losing him than being recognized. He assumed Traculus was leaving the arena, but surprisingly, he was not going up and out, but down.

Atticus struggled to weave his way through the maze of fortune-telling stands, freak shows, souvenir sellers, sausage vendors and the boisterous milling crowd that jammed the area under the stands.

He kept pace as Galerius Traculus descended even farther, down into the rabbit warren of subterranean tunnels that ran under the arena floor. Traculus moved quickly past the dressing area where the gladiators would, when their day came, prepare. He strode purposefully past the elevators that were attached to the counterweights and pulleys that would bring the wild beasts up to the surface from their underground cages.

The air was noxious and stifling. Galerius Traculus stopped long enough to catch his breath and wipe the sweat that was streaming down his fleshy face.

Atticus's eyes stung from his own salty sweat. But giving up never crossed his mind, because the feeling that something was about to be revealed intensified with each passing moment.

When Galerius Traculus abruptly turned a corner

that led to a dimly lighted corridor, Atticus feared he had lost his man. He took a moment to focus and was relieved when he was able to make out his gargantuan shape only a few feet in front of him.

He was waiting for someone. But who? Atticus thought. Galerius Traculus had felt safe enough meeting the four men upstairs in the arena, so who could it be that he had to meet down here, where no one could possibly see them?

Atticus remained absolutely still, barely breathing, his back pressed tightly to the muddy wall. It was silent except for the drops of water dripping from the ceiling onto an abandoned, overturned shield lying on the ground. *Plink, plink, plink* — the drips were keeping time with Atticus's racing heartbeat.

Someone was there; in the shadows, he could see movement. They moved ever so slightly out of the darkness into a narrow shaft of light.

So much did Atticus not want it to be who it was that he nearly succeeded in convincing himself it wasn't. But the truth can always be distinguished from all else.

He watched, so stunned he had to stop himself from crying out.

They came together, standing nearly cheek to cheek so that they could whisper in each other's ear. There were only a sentence or two that Atticus couldn't hear. Galerius Traculus handed her a purse he had tied within the folds of his toga. Then they parted, Galerius Traculus brushing past so near Atticus that they almost touched.

Moments later she left, coming just as close to Atticus. What his eyes had seen but didn't want to believe, the subtle scent confirmed.

Lady Claudia's perfume was as distinctive as it was exclusive. Atticus had witnessed enough conversations with her perfumer to know that it had been conceived for her alone. He lived with it day after day, and even when she was gone, the smell lingered. There was no mistaking it.

His master had instructed him that there would be four men, clearly unaware of the secret rendezvous between Galerius Traculus and his wife.

His master had expected nothing, but now he would know the truth.

Atticus had never been afraid of his master, even from the very first. But now he was. He knew he was the bearer of bad news and he didn't know how Lucius Opimius would react.

As always he reported in detail, and when he got to the end did not hesitate. Lucius Opimius turned from him and walked away, thinking, but also, Atticus thought, not wanting to reveal himself.

After a moment or two he turned, now composed, came toward Atticus, bent forward and put both hands on his shoulders. "Good job," he said. "You did what you had to do."

HE SEEMED, LIKE FINE WINE, TO GET BETTER WITH AGE

❖ ◆ ❖ ◆ ❖

Lucius Opimius never made a decision, certainly not an important one, without consulting Aristide. Aristide had been born in Athens, educated in Alexandria and could speak and read Latin as well as Greek.

Master Lucius believed it was foolhardy to proceed with anything of importance without looking to the gods for direction and seeking signs from the heavens.

Before making his recommendation Aristide would carefully review the positions of the planets and the stars at that particular moment and, taking into consideration Lucius Opimius's birth chart, make his final recommendation.

Lucius Opimius had first employed Aristide

many years ago when he was a young, ambitious advocate on the rise. Whenever there was a pending bill, an important speech or a crucial day in court, he would ask Aristide to observe the sky and advise him of any omens or signs: lightning striking a particular building; a statue inexplicably falling from its base.

Time and time again Aristide urged Lucius Opimius to postpone his actions until the planets were in a more propitious position. And always Master Lucius heeded his advice.

Unlike others, who dismissed their astrologer not only if his predictions failed to come true but also if they merely prophesized unpleasantries, Lucius Opimius stuck with Aristide even when he was in error.

Aristide's record in recent years, however, was remarkable. He seemed, like fine wine, to get better with age. He had accurately foretold that Larcius Licinus's first wife would go to a watery grave on the last day of Kalends. On the date specified her covered litter overturned while she was traversing a bridge and dumped her into the raging river below, where she was swept away by the swift current. All this while her husband was busy sleeping off another marathon night of wine drinking. The rest of her party looked on horrified but utterly helpless: She was never seen again.

Perhaps even more impressive he had predicated, after seeing a lone wolf skulking down a side street howling at the full moon, that Avidius Ariston would be murdered by his wife (who reportedly said, upon her arrest, enough is enough, although no one, not even Aristide, knew precisely to what she was referring).

Lucius Opimius seemed to rely on Aristide more with each passing year. Some, the physician Cassius Macedo and Lady Claudia prominent among them, believed that Lucius's growing reliance on Aristide had gone to the astrologer's already too big head.

If this was true (its veracity was not at all certain, jealousy being the most common of a man's many character flaws), it could not be seen in Aristide's kindly face.

It was, even his detractors had to admit, an invariably honest face: soft brown eyes and a sorrowful countenance combining with his thick beard to complete a picture of perfect benevolence.

His detractors believed that it was merely a façade, hiding a lust for power obtained through his witches' brew of astrology, omens and signs all employed to manipulate gullible Lucius Opimius to eventually do Aristide's bidding, although no one was quite sure what that might be.

It Was As Though He Was Being Drawn There By an Unseen Magnet

❖ ◆ ❖ ◆ ❖

It had been years since Lucius Opimius had spent the summer in Rome. The only question was which of his country villas he would go to: the one near the port of Ostia, the one at Arpinum or the one in Capua.

As early as the Ides of March Lucius would begin to count the days. He loved the city of his birth, and couldn't imagine living anywhere that would be more stimulating. There was much, however, that he was glad to leave behind, at least for a few months: his power-seeking peers and their status-conscious wives; the constant babble of the mindless mob; the incessant and ever-increasing traffic and street noise; the fear of fires that was as real as it was terrifying; and the odious, oppressive summer heat.

Of course the most important benefit of leaving was that, once beyond the city limits, Lucius Opimius no longer had to wear his accursed toga.

And he was not going to repeat the mistake he had made last year when he returned too early. That only proved that September could be as bad as June, worse even, especially when one considered the fevers that invariably raged.

Besides, the senate was on vacation in September, so it was a time when very little happened in Rome.

Oddly, and most uncharacteristically, Lucius Opimius did not consult his astrologer as to which villa to go to or the most appropriate departure time. In fact, the announcement that he had chosen Capua, which pleased everyone, was followed by the startling information that they must be ready to leave by the next day.

This news electrified the household. Usually it took weeks to prepare to leave for the summer. Now they were to do it in a day. The house became a bee-hive of activity, everyone buzzing off in all directions at once, but each one with a purpose.

Atticus was excited about the upcoming journey

for reasons of his own. His master had announced that it was time Atticus began his education. Under Aristide's tutelage Atticus was to learn, rhetoric and writing. Master Lucius hoped that eventually Atticus could become proficient enough at writing to take dictation from his master.

Somehow, by the next day, everything was ready for the journey. Lucius Opimius suggested that it might be wise for the new student and his teacher to ride in the same carriage during the journey to Capua.

Aristide's carriage traveled, for a while, side by side with Lucius Opimius's four-wheeled carriage, which contained the master, Lady Claudia and Cassius Macedo. The good doctor was originally going to remain behind in Rome, but at the last minute, it was thought best that he attend to Lady Claudia, who was feeling poorly.

Cassius Macedo dutifully saw to the packing of the various cures he had been using to help Lady Claudia with her frequent illnesses and to calm her nerves: rosemary, sage, garlic, fennel, red cassia, seed of hazelwort and victoriatus of myrrh. None, however, seemed to offer any relief, as she seemed even more skittish than usual recently.

Travelers coming from the opposite direction, seeing the apparent wealth and distinction of Lucius Opimius's procession (he was bringing more than forty slaves with him to Capua, even though three hundred slaves were there already) stayed to the side of the road, respectfully offering them the right of way.

They rested and refreshed their horses and themselves at various public houses along the route and made good time. Atticus and Aristide rode in silence, Atticus passing the time counting the milestones that marked the way.

Atticus still felt uneasy around Aristide, even though he had come to know him more and more over the past few weeks.

At first Atticus had dismissed him as simply an old fool. He was always gentle and courteous toward Atticus, as he was with everyone, but he was rather an odd bird. He had a strange habit of muttering to himself what Atticus and most others assumed to be a ceaseless stream of indecipherable random remarks.

After a while Atticus began to find excuses to go up to the third floor where Aristide's was the only room. He wasn't quite sure why he was doing it. It was as though he was being drawn there by an unseen magnet.

Aristide liked to spend most of his time up in his room. Invariably he could be found working at his stone table, beneath the window that let in the early morning light. He appeared to be completely lost in thought, his head bent over the table doing complicated calculations with a piece of charcoal; working furiously on his abacus; or scribbling away on his wax tablet, constantly cutting the nib of his reed pen until it was sharpened to his satisfaction.

Atticus would hurriedly walk past Aristide's room, trying to give the impression that he was tending to something urgent. He did this so many times that finally, Aristide, without lifting his head from what he was doing, muttered into the dense thicket of his long, salt and pepper beard: "You don't have to walk past, you know — you can just come in."

Once the invitation was accepted, Aristide seemed content to return to his work, acting as if Atticus wasn't even there. Atticus, for his part, was too afraid to utter a sound or even move.

Looking at the room he realized there wasn't

enough space to really move around, and certainly no place to sit. Aristide occupied the only chair, and every inch of floor space, indeed the whole room, was filled with clutter: writing paper new and used; books piled up halfway to the ceiling; wax tablets covered with writing; papyrus rolls stacked along and covering one wall; a sundial that had no business being inside where, without the sun, it was obviously of no use; and leftover bits of dinner — bacon, stuffed derma, sardines and stale bread crusts.

Atticus fell into the habit of going up to Aristide's room each day after he and his master returned from the baths and marketing. He began to feel more comfortable and, as a consequence, paid closer attention to Aristide's ongoing muttering monologue.

It wasn't what it appeared to be, at least not all of it. Yes, most of it was idle chatter about various concerns of Aristide's: why paper cost so much more than parchment, why books were so costly and why they took so long to hand copy, how he was going to preserve his precious library of rare books, and so forth.

Occasionally, however, these seemingly inconsequential utterings were interrupted, without warning, by statements of a weightier nature. When Aristide came to one of these pronouncements, he spoke a little more slowly, a little more deliberately. It was as if he were carefully considering whether this was *precisely* the word he wanted to use. Wondering if, perhaps, another word might more accurately communicate the thought he wanted to convey.

It was as though when he came to those statements, speaking out loud was a profound and abiding commitment.

Atticus came to realize that he had been fooled by Aristide's eccentric ways. His muttering and offhand style of speaking camouflaged the true wisdom of the words. He even suspected Aristide of playing a subtle game. Testing to see if, despite the informal delivery, Atticus would be able to recognize the true value of the words. To see if he would realize that they were not worthless coins thoughtlessly tossed aside but precious gems, painstakingly mined, that should be prized and hoarded.

Atticus came to believe that these offerings were nothing less than Aristide's philosophy: his thoughts on the nature of man, his place in the universe and the meaning and purpose of life.

Atticus came to realize that these insights might serve him well in later years, and he dedicated himself to committing them to memory:

- Always treat your so-called inferiors as you do your so-called superiors.
- All men are brothers and by their nature desire freedom.
- Freedom depends on the mind and spirit, not such accidental and ephemeral distictions as birth, wealth and social status.
- Approach all things with seriousness.
- Concentrate fully on the task at hand, avoiding all distractions.
- Always hold your head up high.
- Be strict with yourself and forgiving when it comes to others.
- Be calm.
- Be brave.
- Life must be lived in harmony with nature.
- To live is to be awake.
- Don't waste time. Time is a river. It rushes past and is soon gone.

Atticus found Aristide's words challenging and disturbing. Challenging because he didn't know if he would be able to live up to them. Disturbing because they reminded him of his father, who also insisted that Atticus face the difficult task of living with purpose and intensity.

SUN IN VIRGO, MOON IN LEO

❖ ◆ ❖ ◆ ❖

On the first afternoon of the journey to Capua, Aristide asked Atticus if he would like him to construct his horoscope. Atticus had always been curious about all the calculations Aristide made, charting the position and movements of the planets, and said yes.

Aristide needed to know not only the day and year of Atticus's birth, but the precise time. Although Atticus knew the day — September 22 — and the year — 82 B.C. — he didn't know the time.

Aristide looked disappointed and patiently explained that he would therefore not be able to determine Atticus's rising sign. There was, however, much that could be revealed simply by looking at the position of Atticus's sun and moon.

The next morning Aristide announced that he had finished casting Atticus's horoscope and without waiting for a word from Atticus gave a brief introductory lecture on astrology.

The stars, he said, were powerful deities, and if their characteristics were truly understood and their relationship to each other interpreted properly, they could tell us much about ourselves, the courses of action open to us and our destiny.

It went on like this for quite a while. Atticus nodded from time to time, not wanting Aristide to know that he was understanding as little as he was and that Aristide's lecture was giving rise to more questions than it was answering.

If our destiny could be seen in the position of the stars, why bother to get up each day? Wouldn't your destiny unfold as foretold in the stars even if you remained in bed? Couldn't you, knowing your destiny, then do something to avoid your fate? Atticus wanted to ask the astrologer all of these things but didn't know quite how to start. Aristide's voice was having an almost hypnotic effect on Atticus, as though he were in a trance.

Finishing the introductory lecture and interpreting

Atticus's silence as understanding, Aristide began his interpretation of Atticus's birth chart.

"Sun in Virgo, moon in Leo. You are idealistic and romantic. A person of unquestioned character and absolute devotion to duty. You will serve your master well and faithfully, as I advised him the day he purchased you. He has, with my help, chosen wisely, as he usually does.

"You are committed to the path that is both virtuous and right — a path from which nothing will deter you. You are honorable to a fault and will not cease your efforts until you have dispensed with what you perceive as your obligations.

"You long for recognition but refuse to lower yourself and participate in the maneuvering and scheming that is necessary in the unjust outside world.

"You insist that people come to you and refuse to seek their help. This is a troubling aspect of your personality and may act as shackles on your hopes for your future. You would do well to reconsider this aspect of your personality. It may cause you disappointment and pain in the future if you do not overcome it."

Atticus had wanted to interrupt numerous times. There were so many questions he wanted to ask. He was unsettled by how well Aristide knew what he felt inside, feelings he thought he successfully hid from others. He was unnerved by the realization that there was so much he could learn from Aristide.

But the question he most wanted to ask the astrologer was the question he was most afraid of asking, afraid because he wasn't sure he wanted to hear the answer.

Dreams, Aristide had once told him, were omens that foretold the future, although in ways that were not clear or apparent.

What then, Atticus wanted to know, was the future foretold in his painful, still recurring dream?

It was as if he had spoken the thought aloud, although he was certain he hadn't. As difficult as it was to believe, Aristide was answering Atticus's unasked question.

"As we speak the planets are in a most unusual and favorable conjunction," he said. "Soon you will be facing a grave and profound moment in your life. You will have to look to others for help.

"I have every expectation that you will do what is required of you. I have every expectation that the promise of the dream that causes you such nightly turmoil and torment will be fulfilled."

A Dedicated Follower
of Fashion

❖ ◆ ❖ ◆ ❖

There was one thing Lucius Opimius
didn't consult Aristide about. In fact he hadn't
informed anyone except the messenger he had
personally dispatched, just before dawn, and only
hours after (against his better judgment) giving in
to his wife.

Lady Claudia's requests, in the face of her husband's steadfast refusal, had turned into tearful
pleas. Lucius hated it when women cried. His first
wife had never cried. The crying was the last straw,
as Lady Claudia knew full well it would be. She had
hoped not to have to use it but knew she would if she
needed to.

The messenger rode hard and informed the head
of the famous gladiatorial school, which was located

in Capua, that they would be stopping there on their way to the villa.

Lucius Opimius had no interest in visiting the school. Once like everyone else in Rome, he had enjoyed seeing gladiators in action. In recent years, however, he had become bored. The current rage for ever bigger and ever bloodier games had grown indecently out of proportion. He was horrified as he watched the street rabble (some with jobs, some without, some with homes, some homeless) just go from game to game, barely having a life in between.

Lady Claudia had been, since she was a child, a dedicated follower of fashion, all fashion. And the fashion of the moment was most decidedly gladiators. She knew their names, their various styles of fighting, and who was up and who was down. She was well aware of the famous school in Capua and its reputation for turning out the best fighters in all the world.

She had to admit it took her longer than she had anticipated to extract her husband's reluctant approval. Much longer. And she had had to work harder for it. Much harder. But she had never doubted. She had never even considered the possibility that she wouldn't triumph in the end.

Lying still and alone — Lucius having chosen not to return since dispatching the messenger — she pictured what it would be like.

The gladiators' bodies would be caked with mud, blood and sweat. They would fight to the death, not in the vast impersonal space of the arena, where she was only one of tens of thousands of spectators, but within the small confines of an elite gladitorial school's arena. A combat to the death that was to be put on for her own, very private amusement.

The very thought of it thrilled her to the bone.

She was certain that withholding her plans from her husband, her plans to request not only a private showing but a battle to the death, was the right way to proceed. She was certain that springing it on him, at the last minute and most important in public, where he would be too embarrassed to deny her, was just the right touch.

The Most Dangerous Game

❖ ◆ ❖ ◆ ❖

When they arrived they were warmly welcomed by the lanista, who oversaw the recruitment, training and selling of the gladiators.

Quintas Crassus was the most powerful lanista in all of Rome and the surrounding provinces. He had only this morning been informed by a tired messenger on a spent horse (the last of many mounts he rode) of the pending arrival of his esteemed guests.

Although in truth put off by the short notice — he was used to being treated with more courtesy and respect — Quintas Crassus managed to get everything ready for Lucius Opimius and his entourage, a group he rightly considered visiting royalty.

He announced with a flourish that he had just concluded a deal to send a number of gladiators off to perform in an arena just north of there. That accomplished, he could now devote his full attention to showing this most distinguished gathering that a sumptuous meal was something that, rumor to the contrary, could be had outside of Rome.

Unfortunately the rumors were all too true. Lunch in the noonday sun, despite the shade provided by the awning and the occasional welcome breeze, was inferior in every way, especially culinarily. No one, however, was so ill mannered as to show their disappointment to their most oblivious host.

No one had ever accused Quintas Crassus of being shy, and after boasting about the meal, he went on to boast about his humble beginnings, spectacular rise, and current, phenomenal success.

When he had first gone into business, twenty years before, towns would hire one, maybe two pair of gladiators, and the games they put on would last a day, sometimes two.

Now, happily, all that had changed. Even small towns that could barely afford it were somehow finding the money to build small wooden arenas. They couldn't build them fast enough to satisfy the public.

Now even fifteen or twenty pairs wouldn't satisfy

the crowd. It had to be a hundred, two hundred, and every one had to be a fight to the death. Games went on for weeks, sometimes months. There were even gladiators who were being trained to fight especially on the water, in mock naval battles — two, three, six thousand men at a time.

The public's appetite for death was growing by the day. And the demand for gladiators was growing also, with prices going up and up, with no end in sight.

The lanista, twirling the hairs on his sparse beard and assuming his audience was as delighted with this lecture as he was, went on.

His training school was the largest and most prestigious in all the world, his gladiators the most sought after. He was even thinking of opening another, even bigger school, one where he would train bestiarii to fight wild animals.

He had become a very rich man, he said, with a laugh long and loud (a laugh that, were anyone not to have noticed by now, revealed his vulgarity).

The lanista turned to face Lucius Opimius, who leaned back just slightly, repulsed. He had just this month bought himself a country villa right here in

Capua, and now he could be neighbors with a Roman aristocrat like "my friend here," he said, slapping Lucius on both shoulders.

Lucius Opimius had remained silent throughout lunch, allowing Cassius Macedo and his wife to carry the conversation, which they did most willingly.

Lady Claudia was like an overeager schoolgirl, hopping up and down, unable to remain still in her seat. She had so many questions, she simply could not contain herself, she said apologetically.

Quintas Crassus, who was clearly captivated by Lady Claudia, assured her that her apology was most unnecessary.

Breathless, her bosom heaving with every syllable, she blurted out her questions: What kind of men were they? Where did they come from? What was the age of the youngest? The oldest? Were they all slaves?

The lanista was only too happy to enlighten her.

Yes, many of the gladiators were slaves, he said. Some were sent to the gladiatorial school because they had run away from their masters. Some were sold by masters who wanted to get rid of them, for whatever reason.

Others were common criminals, men condemned to death, who chose the glorious path of gladiatorial combat. Others were innocent prisoners taken in war, or the sons of good families fallen on hard times who had nowhere else to turn.

They were men from Greece, Gaul and Germany. Some were even freemen who were enticed by that most dangerous game: defying death. They hoped to attain fame and fortune but that came only to the luckiest.

Sadly, few gladiators came from the ranks of the Roman legions. The modern Roman soldier wore too much protection and, therefore, didn't really know how to fight properly.

The visitors' timing, he told them, was excellent because a group of recent recruits were being taught rudimentary combat skills at this very moment.

They watched them train with wooden swords and wooden dummies, and fight each other with padded weapons to soften the blows and prevent injuries, until they learned to handle themselves properly. To build up their muscles quickly they trained with weapons that were twice as heavy as the ones they would eventually use in the arena.

They were taught to use their left hands as well

as their right, how to come face to face with an opponent, how to withdraw, how to fight in close quarters, how to attack and feign an attack, which weapons to use when, and not to blink.

Their trainers — retired gladiators, a rare breed since most died during the games — circled around them, armed with a short sword in one hand and brass knuckles in the other.

Next, the lanista said, the group was invited to view the veteran gladiators.

Atticus was amazed by how muscular the men were. Even more muscular than his father and uncle, whose bodies had become as hard as stone after years of working the fields. Their skin glistened with sweat and they moved like wild animals — cautiously, but with stealth and determination.

Quintas Crassus took pains to point out how well cared for they were: tailors made their clothes; they were given massages and baths every day; they were fed a special barley-heavy diet to help build muscles; they were cared for by the lanista's own personal physician, who made sure that their wounds were tended to and that they were in peak physical condition every moment of every day (because one never knew when they might be called upon).

In response to Lady Claudia's request he had the men who represented the different styles of fighting come forward and present themselves for her viewing.

The Thracian, from Greece, fought with a round buckler and a short, razor-sharp dagger. Thracians, the lanista explained, were very much in vogue this year and commanded a commensurately high price. The retiarius fought with a fishing net and a long trident; Samnites carried a shield and a sword.

The lanista explained why metal armor covered their arms, legs, joints, and head, leaving only the chest exposed (where the most truly deadly damage could be done). Each piece of armor was purposely placed to prevent superficial wounds from prematurely stopping the fight before enough toil and blood had been spent.

Now was the time, Lady Claudia decided.

The time to add some spice. The idea just came to her, at the moment. She was amazed that she hadn't thought of it before. It was, she thought smugly, truly a stroke of genius, and it brought a smile to her reddened lips. She would request not only that she be permitted to choose the two gladiators, who would fight to the death right here, right now, but that they fight naked.

THE SLAVE
WHO DEFIED ROME

❖ ◆ ❖ ◆ ❖

"Am I safe in assuming the noble lanista did not mention Rome's most famous gladiator?" Aristide asked Atticus as soon as he climbed back in the carriage.

Aristide had excused himself from the visit to the gladiatorial school, saying he had some important calculations to make and preferred to remain behind in the carriage. Master Lucius, knowing full well the real reason the astrologer wanted to stay behind, had consented.

Atticus was badly shaken by the bloody and brutal battle he had just witnessed: a battle that had no victor. It had ended sadly for both combatants, the "winner" dying of his wounds right before their eyes within minutes of slicing off his adversary's head.

Lady Claudia, who was on her feet from the onset of the contest, applauded frantically throughout and squealed with delight at the "most satisfactory conclusion," as she put it to the beaming lanista.

Atticus was relieved to reenter the otherworldly atmosphere inside their carriage. Even more, he was grateful to be distracted, as they continued on their journey toward the villa, by Aristide's retelling of the legend of Spartacus, the slave who defied Rome.

"Spartacus was a Thracian, just like me," Aristide began. "He was captured and enslaved under circumstances very much like your own, when Roman soldiers overran his village, took what was of value and set fire to the rest, inhabitants included. Unlike you, who had the good fortune to be bought by Lucius Opimius, Spartacus was bought by a lanista and taken to a gladiatorial training school, much like the one you just visited. There he was forced to learn to kill his brothers, to become a gladiator.

"One day," continued Aristide, "he decided he was no longer willing to endure the harsh and brutal training regimen that, despite what I am sure you heard during your visit, was the unbearable reality of his endlessly painful days and nights. He and a handful of fellow desperate slaves-turned-gladiators overcame their stunned guards, killed their hated trainers, grabbled spits, kitchen knives and whatever else they could find and escaped. As fate would have it they happened upon a convoy of carts filled with swords, shields, armor and weapons that they seized.

"They were joined by farmers, shepherds and other fugitive slaves along the way. Word began to spread about the man of enlightenment and vision who was going to lead them to victory over their Roman oppressors and eventual freedom.

"Spartacus was not only fearless but possessed superlative military instincts and a genius for generalship. Time and again his ragged crew, outstanding fighters all — their number eventually grown to seventy thousand — was victorious. Lacking a military base, adequate supplies and proper weapons, they defeated every Roman army sent out after them for two full years. They forced captured Roman soldiers to fight each other in gladiatorial combat, allowing them the opportunity to enjoy the experience firsthand, rather than simply watching.

"In the beginning Spartacus was considered by the powers that be a minor irritation — a pest to be dispensed with using a flick of the hand.

"But a flick of the hand would not suffice.

"All of Rome was astounded by Spartacus's unexpected continued success. Here was a mere slave leading other slaves against Rome's finest soldiers: the Roman Legion. Men who were trained, day in, day out, for years, to be the finest killing machine the world had ever seen — and yet they were defeated time after time.

"The seemingly unstoppable rebellion terrified the citizens of Rome, because it was widely rumored that Spartacus was thinking of the unthinkable: attacking Rome itself.

"Finally, after two exhausting years, Spartacus attempted to escape by sea. But he was betrayed by the pirates who swore to him that their hatred of Rome was as great as his. Their love of Roman money was greater.

"Abandoned and trapped, his back against the sea, he was finally defeated by a huge Roman army sent out to destroy, once and for all, the rebellion that had gone on far too long.

"He, along with six thousand of his men, was captured and then crucified along the road that we are traveling on at this very moment, their lingering, horrific deaths a grim warning to any slaves considering rebellion against Roman rule."

They arrived at the villa just as Aristide was finishing his story. The story had made Atticus forget everything that had gone on earlier.

Neither of them made a move to leave the carriage. Atticus could sense something between them — a vibration in the air. A hum that he could feel but not hear.

Atticus could hear the others, however, who had already begun to disembark, joyous at reaching their destination.

Slowly Atticus turned to look at Aristide, who had already turned toward him. Aristide's eyes had turned silver, the liquid silver of mercury. Atticus had never seen Aristide look like this. He never imagined that anyone *could* look like this. Aristide looked like someone not of this earth.

The astrologer began to speak, but it wasn't him speaking. It wasn't his voice, and the sound wasn't coming from his lips, which weren't moving in the slightest.

It was the voice Atticus had always imagined the gods would use were they to speak directly to him.

"There will come a time when there will be no slaves."

A Jewel in a Most Magnificent Setting

❖ ◆ ❖ ◆ ❖

Although Atticus had heard his master's villa in Capua described many times as a jewel in a most magnificent setting, he was, even so, nearly overcome by the sights and smells that greeted his senses when he stepped from the carriage.

The very air itself was perfumed. Exquisite and exotic scents: oil of roses, essence of lilies, poppies, oranges, sage, mint and sandalwood — all ingredients gathered at great expense from the far corners of the world to be processed at Capua's renowned perfume factories.

The first thing he saw when he walked inside was the extraordinarily large pool in the center of the atrium. Atticus could feel how it cooled the hot air in the room, but its sheer beauty was reason enough for it to be there.

Walking slowly around the pool, ignoring the sounds of everyone running around getting settled, he looked down at his sandaled feet. The floor was artfully covered with an elaborate mosaic illustrating various scenes with snakes, gods, nearly naked women and a bull fighting a bear.

The large room was enclosed by marble columns, ivory, bronze and rare wood furnishings, carefully chosen Greek statues that sat in every niche and corner, and walls that were covered with a lush fresco. The fresco depicted a picnic, the picnickers protected by a large awning, their horses tied to nearby trees while dinner roasted on a spit. As in Rome there were shrines where the family could worship the gods.

There was a library that was even bigger than the one in Rome (and according to Aristide, better stocked and better kept), an ornate private bath and a roof garden where peacocks roamed, making exceedingly hideous noises.

If possible the outside was even more impressive than the inside. The extraordinarily large house sat comfortably nestled on land that seemed to go on forever, every inch of it thoughtfully conceived and lovingly kept. The garden, which contained a carp pool, was lined by poplar trees and included a vegetable and herb garden for the cooks.

The hills sloped down from the front and sides of the villa, and the land was terraced with grape arbors that bore fruit for the villa's much coveted homegrown wine, as well as olive trees for its olive oil.

There was a heated swimming pool, although soon the ocean would be warm enough to swim in, something Master Lucius looked forward to almost as much as not wearing his toga.

On the way to the stables little grottos were located with great subtlety and care so that guests were surprised when they came upon them. Replicas of Greek temples resided within the grottos, and marble benches dotted the white stone paths so that everyone could stop, sit, rest and listen to the water endlessly flowing from the alabaster fountains.

Even the magnificent, surrounding trees that protectively shielded the villa from any invasion of privacy looked more like a pristine park than the natural woods they really were.

We Leave at Dawn

❖ ◆ ❖ ◆ ❖

Everyone was already asleep when the visitor arrived quite unexpectedly. Atticus was only able to get a fleeting glimpse of his purple-accented toga before he was hastily escorted into Master Lucius's bed chamber. But listening to snatches of the conversations as they left the room he recognized the voice. It was that of Senator Caius Curtius, whom Atticus remembered not only from the banquet but from numerous visits and long conversations with his master.

He had come bearing news that must have been of the most dire nature. Atticus could tell by the look on his master's face when he came to him after showing the exhausted senator to one of the guest rooms.

"We're returning to Rome. We leave at dawn. Be ready!" was all he said and all he needed to.

Atticus had been expecting something and he wondered if this was it. He learned, from overheard snatches of conversation as they hurriedly prepared to leave, that Lady Claudia was going to remain behind because she was not feeling well. Cassius Macedo, who would stay with her, didn't think she should make the trip.

Atticus suspected that Lady Claudia's health wasn't the only reason she wasn't accompanying them back to Rome. But his master's demeanor, as always, betrayed nothing, and of course, Atticus held his tongue.

He also learned from these same conversations that they were returning to Rome so that Lucius Opimius could attend an emergency meeting of the senate. Sitting once again beside Aristide in the carriage, Atticus knew that Aristide knew why there was an emergency meeting and why Master Lucius had to be there.

But Atticus also knew not to ask. He had come to learn that Aristide liked to speak when he chose to and reveal only when he considered the time to be right. Were Atticus to ask prematurely, he might jeopardize forever his chances of finding out and, even more important, Aristide's trust.

Anxious and agitated though he was, Atticus disciplined himself to remain silent and still, hoping that Aristide would decide to confide in him at some point during the trip. Hoping he would explain what extraordinary events could cause them to return to the city they had just left.

They were on the road for quite a while before Aristide ceased his mumbling and ended the long silence, the silence that Atticus had filled as best he could with chatter about anything other than what they both were thinking about.

It was late at night, on the day before they were to arrive back in Rome, when Aristide chose to speak.

Signs from the Gods

"I saw three visions.

"All omens, warning of the future.

"An eagle had been released from forced captivity and was bearing someone's spirit to heaven.

"There was an eclipse of the moon, a sign that the gods were angry.

"And I saw a great and powerful storm that suddenly, without warning, turned the city of Rome as dark as night in the middle of the day. There was no chance for people to return home to their loved ones or even to simply run for their lives. They cried out to Jupiter: O most powerful of the gods, save me, but their prayers were unanswered. Trees were tossed into the air, houses destroyed — they vanished in the blink of an eye. Ships at sea were tossed right side up and sank without a trace. Thunderbolts hurled from the sky but the lightning appeared only on the left side of the sky and not on the right, this being most fortunate."

Aristide also spoke of less supernatural events: conspiracies, coups, plots, the welfare of the state and the stability of law. He interspersed heaven and earth with the here and the now, and evildoing with signs from the gods.

Atticus could only hear Aristide; he could not see him. The inside of the carriage was coal black. He thought he saw a silvery glow faintly illuminating the features of his face, but he might have been imagining it.

In the silence that followed, Atticus used the time to piece together what had happened.

A Humble Offering

❖ ◆ ❖ ◆ ❖

There had been a long-planned and well-concealed conspiracy. The object of the plot was to assassinate the Emperor and take over the government.

The Emperor had been aware of the plans since their inception and had subtly and secretly prepared for it.

The attempt failed utterly. The Emperor and his inner circle acted swiftly, surgically and unmercifully.

Although all the facts were not yet known, there were five men involved in the conspiracy. Three were captured alive within hours of the failed attempt. One, General Marius Maximus, had the good sense to attempt suicide by falling on his sword only minutes before he was to be apprehended. He was found by his physician, who managed to effectively bandage his wounds. When the Emperor's men found him, they tore off his bandages and watched him bleed to death.

It was not known who had provided the Emperor with the crucial information about the conspiracy, information that no doubt had saved the Emperor's life and secured the stability of the Empire.

But Atticus knew. His assignments in the barbershop and at the arena. Lady Claudia's startling subterranean rendezvous. And recently, his master's meetings had taken much longer than usual. His conversations in the baths, seemingly casual, were whispered and more intense than ever. And the decision to leave Rome for Capua, with only one day's notice?

Did his master, knowing the time had come, and having set the necessary wheels in motion, remove himself from the scene? Did events move more quickly than he had expected, resulting in the precipitous return to Rome, or had that been part of the plan?

And what of Aristide, who always appeared to have his head in the clouds? Was he aware of all this? Master Lucius never did anything important without consulting him, so what role had he played and how long had he known?

And what of Lady Claudia?

When they arrived back in Rome and Atticus heard who the mastermind and ringleader of the plot was, it all made sense.

Galerius Traculus had initially escaped detection by hiding in a secret vault hidden deep within a subterranean cavern of his home. It was a location unknown to the authorities and even to Master Lucius.

As cunning as he was evil, Galerius Traculus had a fail-safe plan. Were anything to go wrong with the plan he wouldn't flee the city, as everyone would assume. Instead he would hide right there, beneath his own home. No one would ever think to look there. He had plenty of food and water and had paid people well. When they thought it was safe, they were to come and take him away to Greece, where he would decide on his next move.

But there was a flaw in his plan.

Slaves knew everything in Rome. There was constant gossip and constant sharing of information. They knew who was sleeping with whom and who wasn't; who was angry with whom and what they were planning to do about it. This was something to which most Romans, especially Romans like Galerius Traculus, were oblivious.

His slaves, of course, knew about the underground vault.

And they knew he was in there.

Their deep and everlasting hatred of him had been nurtured by years of gratuitous, cruel treatment. Each day they were reminded anew that their lives were worthless.

The only debate was that some of them wanted to seal off the door, which would cut off his air so they could watch him suffocate.

But they lost out.

When it was decided, all of them — women and children included — broke in to the vault and, after cutting off his head, hacked his body into small pieces and fed them to the lampreys in the pool.

Out of love and loyalty to the Emperor a small group of them presented Galerius Traculus's head as a humble offering of their allegiance.

Animal Juggling Act

❖ ◆ ❖ ◆ ❖

The only question that remained was the embarrassingly extravagant, elaborate and expensive games that the Emperor had allowed Galerius Traculus to plan. Games that, were they to go on as scheduled, would be the longest and most expensive in the history of Rome. Games that, had he succeeded in his attempt to overthrow the government, would have announced in grand fashion, to one and all, his ascension to the throne as he crowned himself ruler of the Roman Empire.

The Emperor had already decided that the games would go on. The people, he believed, had been rocked enough by recent events, and canceling the games would just be too much for them right now.

The games would go on, but in a much abbreviated form.

Instead of lasting months they would last days. All preliminary events were eliminated entirely: mock fighting with wooden weapons, fighting from horseback or from chariots, and combat between women. The group of six hundred gladiators, who were already in Rome and were preparing to fight, was reduced to the twenty best.

The Emperor reviewed with disbelief the grossly expensive mock naval battle that had taken a year just to plan. An area adjacent to the main arena was to be flooded, forming an artificial lake three times the size of the arena itself. The lake would be big enough to allow ships, manned by an astounding six thousand gladiators dressed as Egyptian sailors, to make real nautical maneuvers and fight an actual sea battle.

The games had been advertised for months. Many had been looking forward to the naval battle. When word of its cancellation spread, the disappointment was profound.

Even more disappointing was the news that all the events involving wild animals would be limited. At Galerius Traculus's direction, an incredible variety and number of beasts had been trapped and brought back to Rome from all over the world: two hundred tigers from India, four hundred lions from Africa, three hundred leopards from Asia Minor and an untold number of wild bulls from northern Europe.

Some, remembering the Emperor's unfortunate experiences with animal events, were understanding about his decision.

He had been hosting his first games when the lions had inexplicably refused to come out of their cages. Slaves had to be sent in brandishing bundles of blazing straw. Even after being forced out onto the floor of the arena the lions simply lay down. Eventually they had to be killed where they lay by archers stationed a safe distance away.

The crowd, thinking all this was for their amusement, had gone wild.

Later that same afternoon an enormous Indian elephant was struck in the eye by a bestiarius. The eye was rightly considered the best place to strike because the spear might then penetrate to the brains. After falling to its knees, the enormous animal was miraculously able to summon the will and courage to rise halfway up and draw itself toward its tormentors. After piercing them with his tusks, he tossed them in the air as if performing some perverted animal juggling act.

This time the crowd was not amused and neither was the Emperor.

The schedule for the current games was modified: the massacre of wild ostriches and giraffes (two animals never before seen in Rome) by archers, the contest between two elephants, whose tusks were fitted with long iron spikes, and the battle between the bulls and the bears were all canceled.

The condemned man tied to the stake and attacked by starved animals was allowed to go on as planned, however.

An Unwelcome Distraction

❖ ◆ ❖ ◆ ❖

Although Lucius Opimius was deeply honored by the Emperor's invitation to join him in his box for the duration of the games, he decided to attend only on the last day.

There were simply too many "details" in the aftermath of the failed coup that he still had to attend to. Government officials and others who had been involved secondarily in the plot needed to be executed quietly and without fanfare. Others who were deemed disloyal would escape execution but still needed to be removed.

Lucius Opimius considered the rumors about Lady Claudia an unwelcome distraction from his duties. He responded to no inquiries, no matter what the source. His silence, however, only fanned the flames, and there was widespread speculation.

Why hadn't Lady Claudia returned to Rome along with her husband, especially considering the grave crisis he was facing? If she was ill why had her physician unobtrusively, but most definitely, returned to Rome? And, most important, where was she? Was she still in Capua? No one had seen or heard from her since the night Senator Caius Curtius had arrived at the villa to summon Lucius back to Rome.

Atticus knew her true fate, and he wondered if she would have been better off had she simply been put to death.

Instead she was, by the Emperor's decree, exiled "deportatio" — mercilessly and irrevocably. Banished to live in lonely isolation forever on the desolate island of Pandataria.

Master Lucius wanted nothing said of this and, outside of the handful who knew, nothing ever was.

Blood, Sweat and Tears

❖ ◆ ❖ ◆ ❖

Atticus had never seen the games. His anticipation was counterbalanced by his apprehension. He was relieved that his master had insisted that Aristide accompany them. Aristide claimed that he had seen too many games, had too much to do, and, just for good measure, threw in that his gout was acting up, but Master Lucius wouldn't hear of it.

In the days leading up to the start of the games Rome's population seemed to increase tenfold. Despite the summer heat, which had arrived on schedule and in full force, and the unsettling news of the failed coup attempt, farmers, peasants and tourists came from far-off distances, streaming into the already overcrowded city.

They set up tents and slept anywhere and everywhere: along the roads leading to Rome, on the city's main streets and side streets and even on the apartment building rooftops.

So many people were attending the games that it seemed to Atticus that there must be no one left in all the rest of the world.

The games were also well attended by Rome's rich and famous. It was the place to see and be seen. Many arrived in litters carried aloft by their slaves and preceded by African runners dressed in white tunics.

They were accompanied by their wives and mistresses (sometimes both and sometimes together), whose elaborately constructed hairstyles were upstaged only by their jewelry and their overly rouged faces.

The stands were filled to overflowing by the time Atticus, Aristide and Lucius Opimius entered the Emperor's box. Lucius nodded to the consuls, magistrates, senators and other distinguished guests who filled the rows directly in front of the box. They had stood as one when he arrived, to honor him for his recent deeds.

Atticus was grateful he didn't have to sit in the

upper tiers with the farmers, peasants and women. Of course there were a few women in his section — the ladies attending with the Emperor and other powerful men of Rome, and of course, the Vestal virgins.

It was standing room only in the upper tiers and even hotter than down where Atticus was sitting. The large canvas awning pulled across the top of the arena helped block some of the sun's rays but couldn't hope to keep out all of the sun's heat.

The air smelled rancid and foul after days of blood, sweat and tears. Even the perfumed water they sprayed on themselves and the handkerchiefs filled with rose petals that they pressed to their nostrils could not disguise or transform the noxious odor.

Aristide viewed everything through a concave emerald that he held up to his eye, improving his poor vision. Sensing that Atticus was staring at him — Atticus had never seen Aristide use the emerald before — Aristide laughed and said, "Ironic, don't you think, that I can see the future but not the present?"

He answered all of Atticus's many questions about the wild animals while Master Lucius patiently greeted the continuous line of well-wishers who were filling up the adjacent aisles, waiting to pay their respects.

Clearly, word of Lucius Opimius's behind-the-scenes involvement had leaked out.

The animals, Aristide said, were kept below, along with the waiting gladiators, in vast underground cellars. Once the show began, their cages were lifted upward by a system of pulleys and chains, and once at field level, the trapdoors opened and they were let out.

The astrologer assured Atticus that the animals could not attack the crowd. He pointed to the smooth, high walls that acted as a barrier; they were too high even for the big cats to get over. As a backup there was a second barrier of rotating cylinders between the field and the seats that would further prevent the animals from gaining any footing. And lastly, even if, inconceivably, all else failed, there were nets strung up all around the arena.

"Romans," Aristide remarked, "want to be close to the action, not in the action."

THOSE ABOUT TO DIE
SALUTE YOU

❖ ◆ ❖ ◆ ❖

After the animal acts, a fanfare of trumpets heralded what the crowd had been waiting for: the coming of the gladiators.

The anticipation of their appearance alone was enough to drive the crowd to its feet. The gladiators rode into the arena on chariots, made one full circuit, climbed down and marched around, waving to their fans, who shouted out the names of the famous ones.

Then they assembled in front of the Emperor's box, proudly displaying themselves in full battle gear: brightly polished silver arm and leg shields (some studded with jewels and precious stones) and orange helmets (some with peacock feathers waving in the wind). They raised their right arms high and repeated in unison: "Hail, Emperor, those about to die salute you."

One of the Emperor's attendants inspected their weapons. Any that were considered blunt or had the slightest flaw were discarded. Only those with razor-sharp edges were approved.

The trumpets sounded again, signaling the first fight. They sounded each time a man fell, but as the day wore on, the trumpets could barely be heard above the crowd as they shouted out instructions and encouragement.

Fighters who grew weary or tired were lashed with leather whips and prodded with red-hot irons, the intensity of their fighting soon improving.

Swords flashing, steel clashing, one by one they fell, their abdomens slashed open, internal organs exposed and spilling forth rivers of blood that spread out and soaked the sandy soil, which was immediately covered with fresh sand to absorb the blood — remnants of lives no longer lived.

The fallen were also poked with hot irons to make sure they weren't faking, the stretcher bearers carrying out the apparently dead. Down below, those found still alive had their throats cut. Their armor was taken off them, their weapons pried loose from their still gripping, powerful hands and they were piled on carts to be thrown later into nameless, common graves.

And all the while fresh pairs of gladiators were sent in to entertain the crowd with their deaths.

It Was Only a Question of Time

❖ ◆ ❖ ◆ ❖

As dusk turned day to night and the rising dust created a thick, yellow haze that made it difficult to see, only two gladiators remained still standing on the burning, bloody floor of the arena.

They had been evenly matched.

One was a tall, helmet-less, shaven-headed retiarius. He was the biggest man Atticus had ever seen, surely standing seven feet. His body seemed not of flesh and bone but stone and steel.

He was armed with a dagger that he tucked into the belt that held his tunic, a long trident and a fishnet to which a cord was attached so that he could draw it back at will after he ensnared his adversary. He was standing tall, leaning on the trident, which he had stuck in the ground. He was smiling and seemed to be daring the man opposite him to make the first move.

His opponent, although much smaller, was a muscular swordsman. He held his small round shield waist-high and his long sword arched over his head, as if accepting the dare but cautiously awaiting the right opportunity. His face was hidden from view by his visored helmet.

Both fighters had fought long and hard, displaying great skill, superhuman endurance and indomitable will. Those who had been watching them, which included Atticus, Aristide and Master Lucius, were amazed that no one had yet struck a fatal blow.

It was only a question of time, and the gods. Who would the gods smile on, allowing them to survive and fight another day? Live another day?

During the marathon struggle the crowd had come to appreciate their ability to fight, but they would appreciate even more their ability to die.

Now, the crowd, sensing that they were about to witness something rare, quieted for the first time in days.

The fighters, knowing the end was near for one

of them, circled each other, wisely avoiding any unnecessary movement, conserving energy, waiting for that one golden moment.

Earlier in their epic battle, under the scorching late afternoon summer sun, their attacks had been fast and fierce. Now they were more deliberate, although no less deadly.

They knew each move was potentially their last, and although both were tiring, neither was willing to give in. Each parry was quickly countered, each thrust rejected, each attack rendered harmless.

The swordsman, his arms and legs protected, kept his shield close to his chest, offering his adversary as little of the exposed part of his body as possible.

The retiarius, impatient now to end it, had grown more aggressive, taking greater and greater risks. His net whistled over the swordsman's ducked head and then, in an instant, was brought down to ground level, where it curled dangerously around the swordsman's dancing feet.

The retiarius was quick, but the swordsman was quicker. Each time, he narrowly and nimbly stepped out of the trap.

Once, however, the swordsman, not quite as quick on his feet as he had been earlier, tripped on the net and was momentarily caught. The crowd, driven by its lust for blood, roared as one.

The retiarius, looking almost gleeful, rapidly reeled the net toward him, like a fisherman hauling in a big catch. But the swordsman, like an actual fish caught in a net — and employing the same desperation — managed somehow to wriggle free at the very last moment.

The swordsman too had his chance, knocking the trident out of his opponent's hands with an unexpected swipe of his shield, which he had turned suddenly and surprisingly into an offensive weapon. The crowd cheered in appreciation of this intelligent and adroit maneuver.

But the retiarius reacted well and retrieved it in time, agilely removing himself from harm's way.

It was getting dark and difficult to see, when the swordsman made his mistake.

Catching the retiarius's net with his shield hand, he pulled the retiarius forward. A less determined opponent would have fallen at the swordsman's feet and been at his mercy. But the retiarius, showing remarkable strength, managed to stay on his feet and summon the instinct to counter most unexpectedly.

Throughout the contest the swordsman had been unpredictable, changing tactics, switching his sword from hand to hand, maneuvering sometimes in close to negate the effectiveness of the net, attacking on occasion and holding back, keeping the retiarius off-guard and guessing.

The retiarius had been more conventional, almost predictable, using his net for what it was designed for and prodding and thrusting with his long trident.

Now, suddenly, the retiarius changed tactics.

They came together and clashed, and the swordsman, his shield flashing in a ferocious downward arc, gave the retiarius a crushing blow on the back of his head, a blow that, for the first time, momentarily stunned him.

The swordsman, knowing he had no time to waste, moved in to finish him off with one slash of his razor-sharp sword.

Years of fighting for his life had honed the retiarius's instincts to a fine edge. He saw his opportunity and knew that this was his golden moment. Most unexpectedly he dropped his net and grabbed the shaft of the trident with both hands. He swung the forked end furiously around in a wide, ankle-high circle, knocking the unprepared swordsman off his feet on the first rotation.

The swordsman attempted to roll away, but the retiarius drove the forked end of the trident deep into the back of his exposed left thigh. He immediately withdrew it, preparing for another, this time fatal, thrust.

There was a roaring in the swordsman's head, and all before him was black as night.

Valiantly, accepting his defeat, the lower half of his body drenched in his own blood, the swordsman shakily rose to one knee. He managed to steady himself and lowered his head, exposing the back of his neck. He hoped that the retiarius's aim would be true and that his death would be merciful and quick.

Inexplicably the retiarius hesitated, violating a sacred rule: Do not spare your opponents — the man you spare one day in the arena may be the one who takes your life the next.

The retiarius, his face drained of all emotion, looked up at the Emperor's box.

The roar of the crowd had reached a deafening crescendo. All were standing, all were screaming, most in a state of utter frenzy.

Some had their arms extended and their thumbs down, demanding that the swordsman be executed.

But just as many had their thumbs up, beseeching the Emperor to reward the swordsman for his efforts and spare him.

The swordsman, surprisingly, removed his helmet and seemed to look in the direction of the Emperor's box.

He was not appealing for mercy, as other, losing fighters had done throughout the afternoon. He did not raise his left hand and extend one finger, indicating an inability to continue to fight and a plea for clemency.

He was not asking for mercy, but saying, If you want to see me die, know who I am first.

Atticus had been watching the drama unfold with a growing sense of dread. He felt threatened, although there seemed to be no reason for it. He was frightened, terrified even, in a way he had felt before, somewhere in the past.

It was the dream, he realized, shuddering at the thought.

The smells, the sounds, the thick, yellow haze of dust. The approaching darkness. The darkness caused him to be uncertain, only for a moment, of what he now saw before him. But not even the darkness could obscure the familiar face.

"Father!" Atticus screamed as he leapt to his feet.

The Emperor was acutely aware of all that was happening: the evenly divided, hysterical crowd and now, this slave boy calling out. As he had done so many times in the past — more times than anyone other than the two of them knew — he turned to his trusted boyhood friend, Lucius Opimius.

Miraculously the crowd quieted. A vast arena filled with more than fifty thousand bloodthirsty Romans and now, the only sound that could be heard was the voice of a twelve-year-old child calling out for his father.

It might as well have been like that.

For Lucius Opimius, Atticus's frantic cry was truly the only sound he heard.

Lucius Opimius knew his destiny was being laid before him. He didn't need to think. He didn't need to look at Aristide — he had seen the liquid, silver eyes before.

He nodded to the Emperor, who stood, and for the first time all day, gave the thumbs-up sign, bestowing the blessing of life on Atticus's father.

Time Is a River

All of Rome considered Atticus and his father heroes. Atticus's role in recent events was slowly coming to light, although Atticus himself said nothing. Overnight his father had become Rome's most famous gladiator, although he would fight no more, having been pardoned by the Emperor, as was his valiant adversary, the retiarius.

Atticus continued his education under Aristide's watchful eye. He was already proficient enough with his writing to take dictation while his proud master strolled around and around the atrium pool. His father's skill as a toolmaker and blacksmith came in handy, and his almost unearthly way with animals was admired by all.

The days ran into weeks and the weeks easily into months as Atticus and his father became welcome and vital members of Lucius Opimius's household.

Walking one day that next summer Atticus looked up at the sky. It was clear blue — as blue as the sea, dotted only occasionally by a wispy cloud. Atticus could barely believe his good fortune and silently thanked the gods for returning his father to him and allowing them both to find safety and serenity in the service of Lucius Opimius.

But time is a river, as Aristide taught, and it indeed rushes past and is soon gone. Nothing remains as is.

Once again the messenger came late at night, and once again the news was bad.

Aristide, who had observed that very day two eagles fighting directly over his head, besieged Lucius Opimius to come with them to Capua, as planned. But no matter how hard he tried, his master refused, insisting he had to remain behind in Rome because of "pressing business" and promising he would join them in a few days, a week at most.

There had been rumors again, and Lucius wondered if there would ever be a time when Rome was free from her enemies within. He had taken extraordinary precautions, even having all of his food cooked only by his longtime loyal chef. But somehow he was poisoned — the soup was suspected to be laced with lethal leek juice. This was confirmed when his heart failed to burn on the funeral pyre, clearly indicating the use of poison.

Most believed it was an inside job — Lucius was too vigilant for it to be otherwise. The coincidental disappearance of the physician Cassius Macedo, and the rumors that money had bought him heart and soul, pointed to him as the culprit.

The Emperor, grief etched on his face, seemed to have aged in a matter of hours. Miraculously he somehow managed to conduct the affairs of state with his ever steady hand. He publicly warned those responsible for the murder of his dearest friend that he would not rest until they were found. Privately he warned those loyal to him to be on their guard.

Atticus felt as if something inside of him had been torn out. He felt the loss physically. Perhaps as hard to bear was seeing the sorrow in Aristide's eyes.

The astrologer had known the time of trial was not over for Lucius Opimius. But he had been unable to persuade his beloved master to avoid the fate Aristide feared. In his mind the astrologer knew it was a fate his master had to face. In his heart he believed he could save him from it.

They would have to leave, this much Aristide knew. The assassination of Lucius Opimius was a calculated, cold-blooded political act. It would not end there.

By daybreak they were ready. All three — Atticus, his father and Aristide — were unaware that they were changed men. Even in death Lucius Opimius's benevolence shined down upon them. His will, which was read in public by Senator Caius Curtius, stipulated that they were now freedmen. They were also unaware that he had bequeathed his entire fortune to Atticus.

Atticus's father had readied the horses, and

Atticus had packed the food and clothes. Aristide was occupied mapping out their route.

They would go south, like Spartacus, to Brundisium on the coast. There they would find a ship and go to Greece. To Athens, where Aristide was born. Perhaps life would be better there.

Historical Note

The great civilization of ancient Rome followed an epic course, one that has continued to shape our modern world. Rome was founded in 753 B.C., and this city's history is marked by periods of tumult and glory and always a relentless violence. The Romans made contributions to so many aspects of life — religion, architecture, politics, art — which remain with us today. Yet, to truly understand this ancient society, it is important to examine the culture of battle and blood that permeated ancient Rome.

The early Romans were determined to create a homeland in what is modern-day Italy, around the city of Rome. In 509 B.C., the Romans formed an army to defeat the Etruscans in the northern lands. After gaining power over the land and its people, the Romans no longer wanted to be ruled by a monarchy, so instead of appointing a single king, they elected two men from the Senate to rule as consuls. Consuls served for one year and were often military generals.

The Romans went on to fight the Carthaginians in northern Africa and then the Greeks, and with each military victory, they took control of the lands and the people there. Early on, the people conquered by the Romans were welcomed as citizens of Rome, but after 265 B.C., the Romans began to auction off the captured prisoners as slaves. And it was the slaves who were taken in wars that were forced to become gladiators.

Gladiator games first appeared in Rome at around the same time as slavery, in 264 B.C. The games were hosted by wealthy nobles or politicians as memorials to honor dead relatives. In these bloody games, combatants were pitted against one another, to fight to the death; and at times, gladiators even faced wild animals. There was a promise of redemption for gladiators: If they fought well enough, they could win the crowd's support and keep their lives — and possibly win back their freedom.

In 73 B.C., a slave and former gladiator named

Spartacus mustered up an army of thousands of other slaves and led a revolt against the Romans. The Romans met Spartacus with a professional army of 40,000 soldiers and put down his rebellion. Spartacus was killed in battle, and thousands of his comrades were taken prisoner and crucified — an agonizing method of execution in which one is nailed to a cross and left to die slowly and painfully. Crosses stretched for miles along the Apian Way, one of Rome's most traveled roads, a gruesome reminder of Roman brutality.

After many wars and a great deal of unrest at home, the city of Rome had grown into an empire, which encompassed provinces stretching from modern-day Great Britain to the Arabian peninsula. The Romans built roads of giant blocks of crushed stones and pebbles that connected far-off lands to each other and to Rome. And some of these roads remained in use until one hundred years ago.

The politics of Rome were not so clearly marked, however. The Roman government began as a republic — meaning the citizens elected their own leaders — that lasted for nearly five hundred years. But, only men with money and property to their names could vote. There were two branches of the

Republic: the citizen assemblies and the Senate, and the Senate was by far the more powerful. Consuls continued to govern in distant lands (as proconsuls), and they often remained military leaders with the power to make war in order to expand the Empire.

However, as Rome plunged ahead in its military campaigns, defeating foreign nations and forcing those populations to bear the chains of slavery, the nobility of Rome grew increasingly wealthy and corrupt and the Republic itself grew weaker and weaker. Labor conflicts, slave revolts, and riots, along with the wars waged by and on other nations, engulfed Rome and made the government vulnerable to a takeover.

Throughout this series of violent uprisings and protests and civil wars, the Republic — senators, noblemen, citizens and reformers — fought to stabilize itself. It was then that the First Triumvirate was able to emerge from the wreckage of Rome and take control of the Republic. Pompey "the Great," a famous general; Crassus, a wealthy nobleman; and Julius Caesar, an ambitious military leader and the consul of Gaul, divided up power, and wrested control of the Republic away from the people and the institutions of Rome. However, Crassus and

Pompey were both killed in battle, and the power became Caesar's for the taking.

He led the citizens through a series of political reforms, yet all of his moves were meant only to ensure his continued power. After Julius Caesar was killed in 44 B.C. by his friend Brutus, who was known as a defender of the Republic, a new power came forward. A Second Triumvirate formed by Julius Caesar's adopted nephew Octavian Caesar, along with Marc Antony and Marcus Lepidus, held the reins of power until 33 B.C., when Octavian defeated Antony in battle. Octavian then became the imperator — from which the word "emperor" is derived — and took the name Augustus, meaning "revered," becoming the next absolute ruler of the city and its vast empire, and paving the way for the period of the Roman Empire.

Octavian lived a moderate life; he inhabited a simple house and did not throw lavish parties. A clever politician, he did not anger the citizens of Rome, and, unlike his uncle, he refrained from making the Senators feel threatened. Octavian allowed the Senate to continue functioning as a branch of the government, but he maintained control of the Roman army and tax collection. He led the Roman Empire into the period known as the Pax Romana, or the Roman Peace, which lasted for two hundred years.

✦　✥　✦

The Romans created many institutions that influenced the course of history. For instance . . .

◆ While the Romans adopted the ancient Greek gods of mythology and renamed them to make them their own, Christianity was born in the Roman Empire, and in 395 A.D., Christianity was the Empire's main religion.

◆ Latin, the language of Rome, made its way across the Empire and became the foundation for many modern languages, such as French, Spanish, Italian and Portuguese, which are known as the Romance languages. English and German also have elements of Latin, and these languages still use the original Latin alphabet.

◆ The Romans took many ideas about architecture from the ancient Greeks, such as the use of columns and arches in buildings. And then the Romans improved on the arch and created the dome, an entire roof formed by rounded arches.

- Though most Romans could not read or write, a large and very significant body of literature emerged from the Roman Empire. Most famous is probably the epic history of Rome, the *Aeneid*, by Virgil.

- As Roman cities grew to become the most populated in the world, water became scarce. So, the Romans invented ingenious methods for carrying water from distant wells or springs into the cities, such as huge stone structures called aqueducts. These were constructed of a series of arches, with a trough running along the tops of the arches to convey the water.

- The Romans invented building materials, such as concrete. By mixing lime and soil and letting it harden as it dried in the sun, Romans created bricks. And architects were able to use these strong bricks to build enormous constructions like the Coliseum.

About the Author

❖ ◆ ❖ ◆ ❖

Barry Denenberg is the highly acclaimed author of many books for young readers, including, *Voices from Vietnam*, which was praised by *Booklist* in a starred review for being "A high-caliber oral history expressly for young adults." He is also the author of *An American Hero: The True Story of Charles A. Lindbergh*; *Nelson Mandela: No Easy Walk to Freedom*; *Stealing Home: The Story of Jackie Robinson*; and *All Shook Up: The Life and Death of Elvis Presley*, all of which received extraordinary reviews. Mr. Denenberg is also the author of *Pandora of Athens*, another book in the Life and Times series.

Mr. Denenberg has written several books for the Dear America line, including *Early Sunday*

Morning; *One Eye Laughing, The Other Weeping*; *When Will This Cruel War Be Over?*; *So Far from Home*; and *Mirror, Mirror on the Wall*; and for My Name Is America, *The Journal of Ben Uchida* and *The Journal of William Thomas Emerson*.

ALSO AVAILABLE IN THE LIFE AND TIMES SERIES

Pandora of Athens
399 B.C.
By Barry Denenberg

AND COMING IN APRIL 2005 . . .

Maïa of Thebes
1469 B.C.
By Ann Turner